Sing to the Dawn

Minfong Ho
Sing to the Dawn

Illustrated by Kwoncjan Ho

Macmillan/McGraw-Hill School Publishing Company
New York ▪ Chicago ▪ Columbus

Macmillan/McGraw-Hill School Division
10 Union Square East
New York, New York 10003

Printed in the United States of America

ISBN 0-02-179538-X / 7, L.13A

  2 3 4 5 6 7 8 9 WES 99 98 97 96 95 94 93

Years ago,
in the fields
outside my window
at home,
a slim girl
in a pale pink blouse
would herd her
water-buffaloes off
every twilight.
This book is
for her.

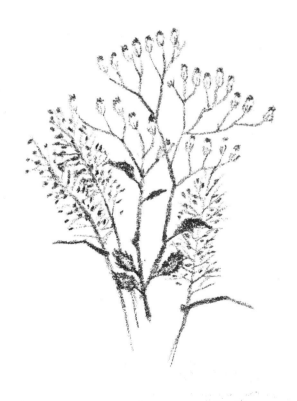

Yaam mau far saang
Nam kaang young oui ing
Fung si-dun don-tri
Bi mai tung kan king
Chum chaen berg-baan ru-tai jing

Dawan raerm song laa
Tong-far yaam arun
Lom choy chuwan
Haun la-hoy soi
Chup chee-wa pasuta dan tong

Sodsai chai rerng ra
Rung far rerm sawang
Loit len bai
Dawan chai young dan din
Tong tung naa ba prai ma-tupoom

Chapter 1

The drizzling of the cool night rain had stopped, and in the calm silence of the after-rain, the deep croaking of the bullfrogs rose and ebbed, like a baby's quiet sobbing. Dawan shivered slightly on her thin rattan mat and opened her eyes.

It was still dark, but in the wet moonlight outside the window she could see the shimmer of raindrops on smooth banana leaves. Propping herself up on her elbow, she looked around her. The sleeping shapes of her family, lying in mosquito nets, were still and peaceful. Nobody seemed awake, not even Kwai, her brother. The whispery gossip of the leaves outside surrounded them all, snug inside the little thatched hut.

Slowly, she closed her eyes again, and listened to the morning noises flow about her. The pulsing croaks of the bullfrogs had died down now, and given place to the fragile first cries of small sparrows. The breezes of dawn, sifting through the countryside, brushed against the wooden shutters of the windows, making them creak gently. Dawan liked this part of the day best of all, when the waves of after-night twined so gently around the slow swirls of before-dawn.

Somewhere in the distance, the crowing of a rooster drilled through the fluid stillness. Dawan smiled. It was now officially morning, and her father could not reprimand her if she got up to wander outside.

Moving quietly so that she wouldn't disturb the others, she rolled up her own piece of thin matting. Then, just as she was crawling out of the mosquito net that she shared with her two sisters, she saw Kwai's head popping out from the mosquito net that he shared with the baby. Dawan grinned. She should have known that her brother had been awake all this time too. After all, this morning was as special to him as it was to her—perhaps even more so.

His round eyes twinkling, Kwai motioned to her to be quiet, and together they tiptoed to the wooden platform outside and scampered down the ladder. The ground was squishy and cool from the night rain and the sky a blue-gold, with a few stars still resting in it. Dawan stretched her lithe body upwards, up to grasp a wisp of air, and almost burst out laughing, it was so fresh and cool and young, this morning!

Hearing a noise behind her, she spun around and saw Kwai racing past her down the small path to the

river. He glanced back once and tossed his head impatiently, as if to say, "C'mon, hurry up!" She darted off after him, weaving her way quickly between the tall leafy trees. The mud oozed through her toes as she ran, and sometimes cool puddle-water splashed up and streaked her bare legs. Shaking the long black hair out of her eyes, she would reach up and grab handfuls of wet leaves, gleefully scattering dew-drops and rainwater everywhere.

The thick undergrowth surrounding the path suddenly cleared, and Dawan stood, breathless, at the edge of the river. The water flowed calmly, with an occasional sparkle gleaming here and there on its surface. She looked for Kwai's head bobbing in the river. But he was nowhere to be seen.

It was beginning to dawn now. The tender green of the newly planted paddy-fields stretched out on the other side of the river, tinted with a tenuous gold. Squinting slightly in the direction of the dawn, Dawan's eyes scanned the horizon. As far as she could see, young rice stalks gently parted and merged in the early morning wind.

Kwai wasn't in the fields either. Finally she looked to the far left of the river, where the old wooden bridge stood gracefully over the water.

And right in the middle of the bridge a small, solemn figure was perched, his legs dangling over the edge. It was Kwai.

Laughing gaily, Dawan sprinted the remaining distance to her brother. When she reached the foot of the bridge, she stopped and shouted. "Kwai, I'm coming up too!" He smiled, and for an answer moved over slightly to make room for her.

Carefully avoiding the holes and loose planks of the rickety old bridge, she climbed up to sit down next to him, letting her legs dangle over the edge beside his.

For a long while neither of them spoke, but sat together in easy companionship, watching the sunglow creep over the awakening world. A coy breeze played with the drowsy countryside, tickling the long blades of the paddy-fields, flirting with the loose strands of her hair, wrinkling the translucent skin of the river water. Dawan felt the deep joy of a new day radiate forth from within her.

Leaning back a little on her palms, she started singing softly. It was her own song, one which she had made up herself, but so gradually and unconsciously that it had always seemed to her that she was born knowing it. It had a fluid, lilting tune and as she sang it, she swayed gently from side to side, rocking herself to its smooth rhythm. Her voice rose up to twine around the wind, teasing the dull rustle of the weeds. And this is what she sang:

> "Misty morning
> mist is lifting,
> melody of trees
> slowly sifting
> through the gold-green branches.

Dappled morning
sun is flying,
breaths of breezes
rising, dying,
brushing over the earth's brown skin.

Happy morning
my heart is singing,
arms spread wide
the dawn is bringing
its sunglow to this land, my home."

As she sang, Kwai also rocked himself back and forth.

Dawan took a deep breath, letting the morning air seep through her whole body down to her very fingertips.

Kwai glanced over at his sister, and said matter-of-factly, "You're happy," and threw a little pebble lying by him into the water. Dawan, gazing at the ripples sent out by the pebble, said just as matter-of-factly, "You make nice ripples." And the two of them smiled into the flowing water.

The sun had risen by now, and was carelessly tossing droplets of light onto the water from the clear blue sky. Sounds of the awakening village were carried over to them—the cries of babies, soft laughter, and cooking noises. The world was finally awake.

"C'mon, Sister, let's hurry home to have breakfast and head for school," Kwai said, standing up. Dawan, however, did not seem to have heard him, and remained sitting there. "C'mon, Sis," Kwai repeated impatiently. Still his sister did not move.

Then Kwai understood, and sat down next to her again. "Is it because today the marks come in and we find out who won the scholarship that you don't want to go? Sister, are you afraid of finding out?"

Dawan stared at the spot in the water where the ripples had been. After a while she glanced at her brother and asked, "What if you did do best in our village, Kwai? You will go, won't you?"

Kwai shrugged and tossed another pebble into the river. "Who can turn down a free education, especially one in the City? If I win, of course I'll go." Behind his easy manner, Dawan could sense the excitement in him.

"If I do get to go, I won't spend all day in school reading old books, though. Remember the big markets Cousin Noi told us about? She said that jasmine buds are sold by the bucketfuls and rows of pigs' heads hang outside the butcher stalls, and countless different kinds of coconut cakes are sold there. I'm going to see for myself what that's like, maybe buy a new flower sarong for Mama or something." Kwai's eyes were shining and, as he spoke, he swung his legs back and forth happily.

"And the temples, too, Kwai!" Dawan added.

"Oh yes, and I'll go to the most beautiful, most sacred temples, the Temple of Dawn, and the Temple of the Emerald Buddha—all the ones you see in Noi's color postcards. I'll even light some incense especially for you, Sister, and . . ."

Dawan broke out laughing. "At this rate, you won't have much chance for studying at all, Kwai!" She glanced at him and continued more seriously, "You know what noble hopes our teacher has for your future, my brother. Don't disappoint him."

Kwai lowered his head and stared fixedly at a small clump of lotus pads resting on the river surface. "Are you sure, Sister?" he asked slowly.

"Sure of what?"

"What you just said. That Teacher has high hopes for me?"

"Not for *you* exactly, Kwai, more for what you will do for all of us. Why do you think he spends hours talking to you after school sometimes, about injustice, and poverty, and . . ."

"Well, he talks to you, too."

Dawan shook her head. "Only because I always wait to walk home with you, Kwai. He can't very well ignore me when I'm standing right in his class-room doorway."

Kwai knew that this was a sensitive point with his sister, and did not pursue it. "I won't be playing around all the time, Sister, if I really do get that scholarship. You know that. You know all the plans I have of wanting to improve life in our village—all those things that Teacher has discussed with me . . ." He stopped abruptly, and corrected himself, "with, with us."

His sister gave no sign that she had noticed his slip, and so he continued, "Teacher said that very useful things are taught in the City school, so if I do go, I'll study hard there, and then come back to teach Father how to raise new crops, and use better fertilizers, or even set up a hospital for our village, or advise the people here how not to get cheated by the tax collector . . ."

"Did you see the sacks of rice stacked up beneath the house this morning, Kwai?" Dawan broke in, suddenly reminded of them by the mention of the tax collector.

Her brother nodded gloomily. "How could I help but see them? There's such a big pile!" He threw a pebble into the river. "Is the landlord's tax collector coming for them today then?"

"Must be," Dawan muttered. "But Father didn't say anything about it. I think he's worried that by the time he gets through paying the rent for the rice-fields, there won't be enough rice for us anymore."

"It's not fair," Kwai burst out, "that we worked so hard all year plowing and planting and reaping, and some landlord, whoever he is, collects so much of our rice without even lifting a hoe!"

His sister nodded vigorously. "And he collects whole piles of rice from *everybody* in the village. What right does he have to take our rice anyway?"

Kwai frowned, then shrugged. "I don't know, Sister. Why don't you ask Teacher about it in class today? He'll know."

"You ask him," Dawan replied quickly, staring at a dragonfly perched on the tip of a lotus bud.

"But why? It's your question." Kwai sounded annoyed. "Don't always be so afraid of speaking out in class, Sister. He encourages us to ask questions. And besides, he likes you."

The dragonfly glided off, its light wings catching the sparkles of sunlight as it skimmed over the river water. Dawan's eyes did not follow the dragonfly, but remained fixed on the lotus.

"He likes you more," she insisted in a low voice. "Especially today, when you will receive the government scholarship."

"Stop talking as if I had already won that scholarship!" Kwai interrupted. "There are plenty of other students in our village who might get it, you know."

"Like who?" Dawan challenged.

Kwai fell silent, as if he was mentally considering every member of his class who might win. Finally he blurted, "How about you, Sister? You could win."

"Me?" Dawan flushed. "But I'm a girl."

"You're older than I am. Maybe they want older students."

Although Dawan was already fourteen, and a year older than her brother, she was in the same class as he was. Their parents had considered it foolish and wasteful to send girls to school. It was not until Kwai had started school himself and kept insisting that his sister be allowed to join him that Dawan was finally permitted to go too.

"Kwai, don't be silly," Dawan said wistfully, "I won't get the prize."

"I'm not being silly," Kwai retorted. "You always get good marks, and you study harder than I do. Why shouldn't you have done better than me in the examination?"

"You know why," Dawan said without looking at her brother, her hands clenched tight over the edge of the wooden bridge. "I'm a girl, Kwai."

Chapter 2

In spite of himself, he smiled. And when he smiled, deep lines radiated from the corner of his eyes and spread out like lightwaves over his whole face, until it seemed that even the tips of his ears were glowing. Tall and lanky, the teacher leaned against the blackboard and gazed at the rows of neatly scrubbed students before him. Not one child was absent, not one was whispering, or even staring out the window. Instead, each face was focused on him, wide-eyed and solemn. His smile lingered on, ebbing away only gradually.

"Well," he said, his usually stern voice tinged with amusement, "what makes you all so quiet today?" Beneath his measured calm flowed an undercurrent of strength, and it was this strength that inspired a fear and respect in his students, so that he never had to cane or scold them.

He nodded briefly, the signal for the class to sit down, and waited until the shuffle had died down before beginning again. "There is something I want to discuss with you today, something which is probably on your minds right now."

There was a hushed expectancy in the classroom. "On your way to school this morning," he continued in his low, firm voice, "I'm sure many of you noticed something different, something unusual beneath your houses. What was it?"

This question was met with only a blank disappointment: surely this had nothing to do with the scholarship. Dawan noticed that her brother frowned, a puzzled and annoyed expression on his face.

"Look, this is really important," the teacher said, frowning impatiently himself. "Put everything else you may have on your mind aside, and think about this for the moment. What did you see beneath your homes this morning?"

He asked his question so urgently that a slight wave of interest, like a breeze through dainty leaves, stirred the students. There was a rustling of soft words, "Rice . . . sacks," "Piles of it . . ." "Our rice . . ."

The teacher nodded. "Sacks of rice. Outside almost every home. Now what is this rice for?"

Finally a boy in the back row raised his hand and stood up reluctantly. "It's rent for the landlord, sir," he muttered, and sat down hurriedly again.

"So," the older man said, folding his hands together, "the rice is for the landlord, and we have to pay rent to this landlord." He spread out his hands again, in a gesture of appeal. "Well, then," he repeated, "why do we have to pay rent to the landlord?"

Now a thin boy in the front stirred, trying to catch the teacher's attention without having to attract that of the other students. It was Takchit, always as conscientious as he was timid.

"Yes?"

"It's, I think it's because the landlord owns the land, sir. We have to pay him rent because we're farming on his land. We're using his land."

"Well, that settles it, then. We pay rent for the landlord because he owns the land." But still he paused, his head cocked to one side, as if awaiting some further comment.

Kwai and Dawan exchanged quick glances: this was exactly what they had been discussing earlier! Kwai saw the indecision on his sister's face and mouthed silently, "Go on! Ask him!"

Hesitantly, Dawan raised her hand. To her surprise, she was acknowledged immediately. She stood up, one of the few times that she had ever done so in class. Acutely aware of her own voice, she asked her teacher, "But sir, why does the landlord own the land? What makes him the landlord? What makes him own all that land instead of us?"

For a long moment, the teacher stared at her in stunned silence. He took a few steps forward, looking at Dawan with what seemed to her to be a fierce interest. Awkward under his scrutiny, she shifted her weight uneasily, yearning but not quite daring to sit down again. He nodded briefly at Dawan, and she sank down to her chair in relief.

Then, pacing across the classroom floor, he said quickly, "Yes, why *does* the landlord own the land? Just what did he do to own the land, this land that we've spent years and years farming ourselves?"

The teacher marched quickly over to his old wooden desk and pulled out the top drawer. He rummaged inside it until he found a piece of chalk, and, armed with that, he strode up to the blackboard. In quick, almost clumsy motions, he wrote one question on the board: "Why does the landlord 'own' the land?" His hands were big and strong, and looked more as if they should be grasping a plow handle than a thin piece of chalk. In the middle of the word, 'landlord,' the chalk snapped in two. Undaunted, the teacher finished the rest of the sentence with the stump of the chalk. Then, underneath his question, he listed three words: "Labor," "Need," and "Inheritance."

That done, he spun around to face his class again, and taking a deep breath, he said, "All right, does this landlord own the land because he has worked on it harder than any of your own fathers have?" He pointed behind him to the word "Labor" scrawled on the board. "Have you ever seen your landlord, back bent, planting rice seedlings all day, or watched him knee-deep in mud, plowing furrow after furrow in the wide fields?"

The interest in his class was rekindled. Most of the students shook their heads, frowning, while a few even snorted. "He's never muddied his hands in his whole life," a big farmboy muttered.

"All right, if this landlord didn't get his land because he worked harder on it than the rest of us," the teacher said, drawing a neat straight line across the word 'Labor,' "maybe he owns it because he needs it more." His hand moved down a few inches and stood poised over the next word.

"Maybe he has a huge family, with hundreds of sick aunts and feeble grandparents to feed. And since they can't work, then of course it is up to us to help him out. We should plow and harvest rice for him to feed them with. Then it's only fair that he should own so much more land than us, because he needs it more than we do."

For a moment there was silence in the room. Then one voice piped up, "But he doesn't *have* hundreds of starving relatives!" That protest immediately released a flood of others. "That's right, he's richer than us!" "Even his servants are richer . . . I saw one with leather shoes . . ." "He wouldn't feed anybody even if they *were* starving!" "He makes *us* hungry!" "He's just a big bully."

"So he doesn't need all that rice, and all that land?" the teacher asked innocently. The shouts of "NO!" were vehement. The teacher looked outside the door uneasily, and motioned for them to quiet down. "All right, then, what does he do with all the rice that he collected from you?"

"He sells it," a sharp voice retorted.

"That's right, he sells it to the people in the City," another student added bitterly. "And he gets richer and richer, just selling off the rice that we planted and reaped!"

"Hmmm," the teacher continued thoughtfully, taking in his whole class in one swift glance. "Then 'Need' isn't the answer to why this landlord owns our land, is it?" Without waiting for an answer this time, he reached out and crossed out the word "Need" on the board.

"So that leaves us with 'Inheritance'," he continued matter-of-factly. "What does that mean?"

Takchit's thin arm shot up eagerly, "It means that his father owned the land, and he got it after his father died."

The teacher nodded, then referred the answer to the class in general, "That's correct, isn't it? This landlord's father *did* own the land."

Seeing a few nods, he continued, "And he did get this land from his father when the old man died?" Again there were nods: everyone knew that this landlord came from a whole long line of landlords.

"If all this is true, then 'Inheritance' must be the right answer." He paused, and, peering down at Dawan, asked her earnestly, "Does that answer your question, child? The landlord owns the land because he inherited it from his father."

Dawan frowned, biting her lip. It would have been easy for her just to nod and agree, but she thought there was something very wrong about the answer. Glancing over at Kwai for support, she mustered up enough courage to stand up and say, "But that word doesn't *explain* anything, sir. It, it just gives the question a name. And it just makes my question . . ." she fumbled for the right way to express herself, ". . . makes the question one step further away. I could still ask why his father owned the land, couldn't I?"

"You certainly could," he agreed, grinning broadly. "And what would my answer to you be then?"

"Only that his father's father had owned the land, and had handed it over when *he* died," Dawan answered quickly.

The teacher turned to the rest of the class, and spread out his hands in a gesture of mock helplessness, "So is 'Inheritance' the answer to our question?"

He managed to quell the roar of "No!" and then turned around to draw a firm line through the third and last word left on the board.

The teacher took a few steps backwards and surveyed the results of his cancellations. "Well, that doesn't leave you with anything for an answer, does it, Dawan?" he asked wryly.

He shook his head, still studying the blackboard. "This landlord didn't work for the land; he doesn't need it, and he doesn't have any real claim on it. And yet," he paused, and it seemed to Dawan that his shoulders sagged a little. ". . . and yet he owns our land. We don't know why, maybe because there is no good reason why, but he owns the land just the same. What is the question we must ask ourselves now?"

Eagerly, without even bothering to raise his hand, Kwai blurted out, "Is it fair?" His eyes were bright and clear as he gazed at his teacher. "We have to ask if giving him all that rice is fair or not."

The teacher nodded quickly. "All right. And is it fair? Well?" he repeated, exasperation putting an edge in his voice. "Just tell me what you think. Never mind if paying rent to the landlord has been the custom for generations. I'm asking you now, is it fair?"

Slowly, a few murmurs drifted up from some of the braver students. "No, no it's not fair." "How can it be?" "It shouldn't be this way . . ." A few even shook their heads guardedly.

"All right then, if it's not fair," the teacher continued briskly, "what must we ask next?"

The class had learned well. This time there was no hesitation. A chorus of softly excited voices answered, "We must ask: does it have to be this way?"

"And does it?" the teacher prompted.

"No, it doesn't," other voices in the classroom immediately answered.

The teacher stepped aside then, and listened with satisfaction to the spirited exchange between the students.

"Should it be changed?" the first group asked.

"Yes, yes it should!" came the emphatic reply.

"Can we change it?"

"Yes we can!"

"How?" the teacher interjected sternly.

The voices subsided, but only for a moment. Then a flurry of hands waved back and forth at the teacher.

He surveyed the eager faces before him, and chose the same big-boned boy in the back row who had volunteered the first answer that morning.

"We could grab the land from that landlord, and then share it between ourselves," the farmboy suggested earnestly. "Then every family would own whatever land it could till. And none of us would have to give up any rice as rent anymore."

"But then your family would have a lot more land than ours would," Takchit complained quickly. "You have four buffaloes and three plows. Your family could till twice the area that my family could."

"Good point," the teacher conceded. "What would you suggest instead, then?"

Takchit frowned, but remained silent. Finally he shrugged, and sat down again.

"We, we could put all our buffaloes and tools in the village center, near the storage bins!" Kwai blurted out.

"We certainly could," the teacher said drily. "But what good would that do anybody?"

Kwai ignored the slight twitter in the class and stood up quickly. "Well, that way everybody could take turns using all the farm equipment," he explained proudly, "so that it wouldn't matter if one family owned more buffaloes than another." He paused, considered for a moment, then added, "The animals and tools would be put to more use too."

The lively discussion continued: how the rice itself

could be shared among the villagers, how a rice mill could be built, so that they could husk their own rice instead of having to pay the middlemen a large sum to do it, how they could pool their spare money together, so that those who needed money could borrow from the fund without having to rely on the loansharks, how . . .

A sudden sharp hiss interrupted the animated flow of ideas. His eyes wide with fear, the boy who sat by the window announced urgently, "He's coming!"

Dawan gasped. Around her voices broke off in the middle of sentences, leaving only a dead silence.

"He" was the headmaster of the little village school. The teacher looked confused for a split second, then, seizing a damp rag, hastily erased the blackboard.

In a monotone, as if he had been speaking that way all morning, the lanky man droned, "Now, you will notice that on page seventy-three of your geography books . . ."

Taking his hint, the students quickly reached inside their desks and pulled out their textbooks. The quiet deftness with which they moved hid the under-current of fear among them.

Each student was aware that the headmaster was peering at them from behind the doorway, but no-one gave the slightest notice of his presence.

Their teacher talked on about the tributaries of Burma and the provinces of Malaysia, in a dull, flat voice, keeping his eyes fixed on his own textbook.

Minutes passed and still the headmaster lurked in

the shadows of the doorway, listening intently. After what seemed to be an interminably long time, the old headmaster nodded approvingly. Then he finally stole away, a satisfied grin on his face.

To play safe, the teacher mumbled on for a while longer, then, sauntering over to the classroom door, poked his head outside and peered around. At the other end of the yard the headmaster was creeping back into his dark little office.

Breathing a sigh, both of relief and of impatience, the tall thin man walked quickly back to the center of the room, and tossed the geography textbook carelessly on his desk.

"Now listen," the teacher said in a deep solemn voice. "We don't have much time left, and I have an important announcement to make. You all know that I received the results of the government examination early this morning. The best student among you will get a free schooling away in the big City school."

An excited murmur swelled up from the class: the scholarship, he was talking about the scholarship at last! Dawan stole a quick glance at her brother, but he had eyes only for his teacher, his whole being taut with suspense.

"Getting the scholarship isn't just winning a prize," the teacher continued sternly. "It also means that the student will be bearing heavy responsibilities. What kind of attitude should that student have towards continuing school?"

Kwai raised his hand hesitantly. "He should learn

what is useful to his own people, and come back to help the village after he has finished learning."

"But how will the student know what will be useful and what will not?" the teacher challenged. "First, that student must learn how to think, to perceive what is wrong with the society, to analyze and understand the rules which create these injustices, and . . ." He stopped abruptly and demanded, "And what?"

"And change it for fairer rules," Dawan whispered softly.

The teacher caught her soft answer. "Yes, and change it for a fairer system," he repeated in a low, solemn voice.

Then, peering down at her, he asked, "Well, Dawan, do you think you could do all that?"

"Me?" Dawan asked faintly. Behind her Vichai snickered loudly, amidst a general round of giggling in the small classroom.

"Well, child?" the teacher persisted, his tone stern but still kind.

Dawan looked up at him in confusion. Why was he deliberately picking on her like his? She glanced around her quickly, and felt as if she was swimming in a sea of wide, taunting eyes.

"Please, sir, never mind me," Dawan faltered. "Just tell us who won the scholarship."

There was a long pause. Distant sounds of a dog barking, of the peasants singing in the rice-fields, of the rustling of palm fronds floated in the open windows. Streaks of gay sunlight darted between the desk and chair legs, forming patterns of light and shadow everywhere.

"But, child," the teacher finally said, his voice sounding far, far away, "you did."

Chapter 3

After the last bell rang, Dawan was surrounded by a crowd of curious and chattering classmates. They bombarded her with loud questions until, shy and reserved as most village girls were, she felt panicky. Gripping the edge of her wooden desk, she looked around desperately for Kwai.

But her brother was not among the crowd. She searched the whole room with quick, frightened eyes until she saw him. He was standing alone in the doorway, clutching onto his pile of dirty schoolbooks and his loneliness, silently watching her in the midst of her admirers.

She called out to him, but he only turned away and stalked out abruptly.

With a knotted feeling in her stomach, Dawan

rammed her way through the crowd after her brother. But in the schoolyard she was again surrounded, this time by the monks that lived in the small temple around the corner.

As she elbowed her way through them as politely as she could, one young monk called cheerfully after her, "Don't forget to tell your whole family the good news!"

That cheerful voice seemed to ring in her ears now, as her bare feet trailed along the path, toward home. "Kwai already knows 'the good news,'" she thought to herself uneasily, "and he hates me for it."

The dew-dampness of the early morning had already dried up in the glare of the hot noon sun.

As she approached the house, she heard the familiar sounds of her mother singing tunelessly to the baby, and of chickens clucking as they pecked the dirt underneath the stilts of the house. Her grandmother was sitting on a tree stump, tired and dignified looking, sprinkling millet for the chickens and watching Dawan's father repair the chicken coop.

"Has Kwai been home yet, Grandmama?" Dawan asked, carefully putting her school books on a low work-bench.

The old woman was about to answer when Dawan's mother walked out onto the veranda above them, her baby balanced comfortably on one hip. She called down to her daughter, "That brother of yours! I don't know what he's up to now! He was here just a few minutes ago, but rushed away again.

37

And he had promised me he'd cut me some bamboo shoots for dinner tonight too!" She shifted her baby up on her hip, then continued, "Dawan, will you be a good girl and help me to . . ."

But Dawan was not listening anymore. She gazed towards the fields, then dropped her eyes listlessly, with a soft sigh.

"Child, is there anything wrong?" her old grandmother asked sharply. She had a way of sensing things, this old woman, and when she spoke like that people usually listened and waited.

Dawan sifted fine grains of dust through her toes, pulled at her earlobes, scratched her knee, shifted her weight from one foot to the other, refusing all the while to look at anybody.

Her father became impatient first and grunted, "Well, Dawan, what is it?"

Dawan glanced over at him and suddenly noticed that the big pile of rice sacks was gone. So the landlord's man had taken everything away already. Her heart sank: her father would be in an even worse mood than usual, making her news that much harder to break. She tried to speak, but the fear in her heart chained down her words.

There were only the sounds of the lazy afternoon breeze in the palm fronds, and of the chickens clucking thoughtfully to themselves. Dawan's eyes flickered over her mother and the baby, at her stern father, and her quiet grandmother, but they finally focused on a shiny puddle by the big brown rain-barrel.

Staring at the puddle, she finally spoke, "You know that prize that the government gives out after the big examination?" Even without looking up she could sense her father stiffen: this meant so much to him too. "Well, the best student," she glanced quickly at her father's unsmiling face and stuttered, "or, or at least the one who happens to get the best marks, well, wins the prize and gets to go to the City and continue to . . ."

"I know all that!" Dawan's father snapped. "What about it?"

In the pause that followed, a tiny green frog hopped out of the puddle onto the dust, his bright eyes blinking at Dawan. The little frog looked so determined and eager that Dawan found strength in it and continued haltingly, "I won the prize. I can go to the City and study some more now." She stole another glance at her father. "Can't I?"

The frog hopped twice away from the puddle, then stood very still, blinking at the vast emptiness of the world about him. Dawan addressed the puddle again, "Please, can I? . . ."

"And Kwai? What about Kwai? He won nothing?" Her father's voice was rough, and yet tinged with a hard wonder. Dawan sensed the pain in her father, and dared not look directly into his eyes.

"There is only one prize," she whispered.

Dawan looked timidly at her father and this time their eyes met and interlocked. There was a long pause, then he spat out, "You took your own brother's chance away from him!" He flung down the hammer he had been holding, and stalked away to the rice-fields.

The grandmother, mother, and daughter all watched him stride away, the silence between them was broken only by the wet plop of the tiny frog jumping back into its puddle. Dawan kept quiet, for she was afraid of angering her other elders. For a while no one stirred, then the grandmother, putting a palm flat on each knee, slowly straightened up from her tree stump, and walked with slow careful steps over to Dawan.

"Child," she said, touching her granddaughter's hand lightly, "I'm proud of you."

Dawan looked up and saw a smile on the dark wrinkled face. She smiled too.

"You should not encourage her so!" Dawan's mother called from the veranda. "You know her father won't let her go. She'll be even more disappointed if you praise her now. At least spare her that."

Dawan felt her heart sinking, not from fear of her mother's anger, but at this suppressed bitterness. Why did her mother sometimes talk as if to hope was a disease, Dawan wondered. How was it that she could be so loving and full of laughter one moment, and then so biting and sour the next. And sometimes, like now, even both at once? Dawan glanced up at her mother, with one plump arm cradling her baby's curled body, the other angrily akimbo. Her moods seemed to be like the contours of her body, one side smooth and round, the other sharp and angular.

The grandmother looked directly at her own daughter. In a voice quiet with conviction, she stated, "I do what I think right."

They continued to glare at each other. Suddenly the baby whimpered, and the mother had to shift her attention to it. The grandmother gave a short grunt of satisfaction, and walked slowly back to the shade beneath the house.

Not knowing what else to do, Dawan picked up her schoolbooks. She was about to climb the ladder upstairs to put her books away in the little corner by her mosquito net, when her grandmother suddenly called her over.

"Child, never mind those books for now," she ordered. "We're going to Noi's house."

"Wait, what are you trying to do?" Dawan's mother asked sharply. "Why do you want to take Dawan to Noi's house?"

The old woman tossed a handful of millet to the chickens, and answered calmly, as if musing to herself, "Noi and her husband have both lived in the City before. They know its ways better than any of us, and can tell us what it is like for a young girl to go to school there. Besides," she added innocently, "they like Dawan a lot."

Dawan's mother squatted down and leaned over the veranda. "I see what you're up to!" she shouted to the grandmother, "You're going to try and talk Noi into arguing for Dawan in front of her father, aren't you?" She brushed a wisp of hair away from her forehead, and Dawan noticed small beads of sweat there. "You think that Noi will trot on over and convince my husband, just like that, to let Dawan go off to the City school? There's no hope in that, old woman! His heart was too set on his son going. He'll never think it right for Kwai's sister, a mere girl, to go in his place."

"Mother, would *you* let me go?" Dawan asked. Her mother did not answer. Dawan repeated her question, "You would let me go, wouldn't you, my mother?"

Still there was only a stubborn silence.

Finally her mother sighed heavily and muttered, "It is not my place to say anything." She turned her gaze back to the baby on her hip, avoiding Dawan's eyes.

"That," replied the grandmother, scattering the last of the millet to the chickens, "is what you happen to think, and that is why Dawan and I will have to walk three kilometers to Noi's home to ask her to speak in your place." She beckoned to Dawan and said crisply, "Come, child, let us be off."

Dawan looked helplessly at the notebooks still in her hands and then walked over to her mother. Standing on tiptoe, she stretched her arm upwards to hand the books to her mother, who automatically reached down for them. "Mother, I am going now," Dawan said, her voice small but determined. To her surprise there was no scolding or protest, not even an acknowledgment of her farewell. So Dawan turned away and joined her grandmother.

The old woman had already started off on her own, a bent figure hobbling step by step along the narrow dirt path towards Noi's house. Dawan sprinted the short distance to catch up with her grandmother.

They had not taken more than twenty steps together when they heard someone calling from behind. Turning around, they saw Dawan's mother running after them in short quick steps, like a frightened chicken.

"Wait!" she panted, slowing down her own pace. Dawan sensed more trouble, and looked up at her grandmother for reassurance. She saw both sternness and amusement flickering behind those faded old eyes. They waited together until Dawan's mother caught up with them. Standing close together in a little triangle, the three of them looked warily at each other.

The grandmother finally broke the silence, nodding to herself and addressing nobody, it seemed, in particular. "Three kilometers is indeed a very long way," she mused absentmindedly.

"Especially under this hot sun," Dawan's mother added quickly, eagerly.

"And I am getting old."

"And you are getting old, Mother."

There was a slight pause and then the grandmother asked abruptly, "Where did you leave your baby?"

"I left him on the ground underneath the house," her daughter answered.

"But there are chickens there," the old woman pointed out. "They might hurt the little one."

"Yes, yes they might. I've seen those chickens some-times peck at his small toes until he cries."

"Well, then, I had better go back to look after him, hadn't I? To make sure the chickens do not peck at his toes."

"Thank you, Mother. That is good of you. And I will walk the three miles with Dawan for you."

"It is kind of you to do that. The way is long and hot."

"And you are getting old, Mother."

The old woman smiled sweetly. "And I am getting old," she murmured, turning away to walk slowly back home.

Chapter 4

Noi's house was cool and dim after the long walk, and Dawan gratefully gulped down the coconut milk that Noi's husband, Ghan, had offered her. The liquid tasted fresh and sweet in her dry throat, and over in the other corner of the room, where the three grown-ups sat in a rough semicircle, Dawan's mother was also drinking deeply from her coconut shell.

The inside of this house was very much like Dawan's own home. It was smaller, but as Noi's family grew, the little house would expand too. Like the other villagers, they would knock down half a wall, and build an adjoining room from whatever rejected old boards were available to them. The special thing about this house, though, was all the colorful postcards and calendar pictures of city scenes tacked onto

47

its walls. It was these pictures of city scenes, of glistening temples and bustling city streets, that Dawan now stared at with bright curious eyes. The thought that she herself might walk through the places in these scenes sent a tingle down her back.

Across the room, the three grown-ups were talking in low tones. Although Noi was only a few years older than Dawan, there was already a small baby suckling sleepily at her breast. When she was Dawan's age, Noi used to giggle and flirt a lot, and was known throughout the village for her daring pranks.

Now, five or six years later, Noi's smiles had grown more strained, and her laughter was somehow soggy. Her voice, too, already held hints of the sharpness that often lurked in the voice of Dawan's mother. Why this was, Dawan could not understand, but she had seen it happen to many young girls growing into womanhood, and often wondered if she would change like that as well.

Dawan gulped down the last of her coconut milk, and put aside the empty shell. She listened more closely to the adult conversation, and heard Noi saying, "But what can a young girl hope to learn, alone in the City? There is nothing good or healthy there, my Aunt. She will only become bitter and angry."

"That is true," Ghan confirmed. "There is no sense in a young girl going off into the City alone."

"But she will be going to school," Dawan heard her mother say. "Surely she will learn much there! This scholarship is really special. She'll never get another chance like it."

"But that's exactly the point," Noi broke in sharply. "She doesn't have to go to the City, does she? She can go to school here."

"What do you mean, Noi? Of course she doesn't *have* to go; neither did you," Dawan's mother retorted.

"I went there to . . . to work, Aunt," Noi said sulkily.

"There's plenty of work to be done in the village," Dawan's mother pointed out, "but you had to go to the City to work!"

"I had to earn money, Aunt. I could earn three times more in the City than any man could earn here," Noi retorted.

"If that's the case," a thick voice suddenly interrupted, "why did you come back so soon?"

A short, flabby man stood outlined in the doorway, his face hidden in the shadows.

Ghan leapt up and strode over to the stranger. "How dare you creep up on us like that?" he asked.

The fat man chuckled an oily sort of chuckle. "There's a lot of things I dare, Ghan," he said.

"What do you want now?"

"What do you think I want, young man?"

Ghan glanced over his shoulder at his wife and baby. "We can talk downstairs," he said curtly.

The stranger turned and winked at Noi. "Of course. After all, it's man's business."

After they left, the hum of afternoon quiet filtered through the windows into the shady room. Dawan's mother frowned, and said to Noi in a low voice, "I thought you two were through with him. I thought that was why you finally came back from the City, and . . ."

"Well, you thought wrong, Aunt," Noi snapped. "We still owe him . . ." she paused awkwardly, ". . . too much. We owe him too much to pay back now."

Dawan stirred hesitantly in her corner. "Who, who is he?" she asked.

Her cousin looked at her in surprise. "You don't know? You've never noticed him prowling around the village before?"

Dawan shook her head.

"He's the army officer who spends his time dragging young men from our villages for the army."

"But why do you have to pay him?"

"Why do you think, child? Because we love him?" Noi said angrily. "Not everything is as it should be. He offered not to draft Ghan if we paid him a sum of money. I was three months with child then and we knew that army pay wasn't enough to feed a cockroach. So what could we do?"

As Dawan pondered this, Ghan called for his wife to come downstairs. Noi got up clumsily, clutching her baby. Halfway across the room she turned around and asked Dawan and her mother to go down with her.

They climbed down the steps silently and joined the two men underneath a palm tree.

Ghan looked at his wife intently and said, "Mr.

Phaspras here has a proposal for us. I want to know what you think about it."

Noi stiffened and held her baby a bit closer to her.

"Now listen, Noi, the landlord already came and took all our extra rice as rent so we don't have enough to pay him. But Mr. Phaspras has offered to let us off until next year, with forty per cent interest."

Seeing confusion in his wife's eyes, Ghan hurried on to explain, "That means if we owe him one thousand this year, we must pay him one thousand and four hundred next year."

"What?" Noi wailed. "But that's so much more! It's not fair! Why should we have to scrape all our money together so he can buy a new radio or a fourth wife?"

"What else can we do, Noi," Ghan asked wearily.

"We could borrow money from someone else until then." She turned to face her aunt. "Maybe your family could spare . . ." she asked awkwardly.

The older woman shook her head grimly. "The landlord's man came around to our house today too. We have hardly enough to last ourselves."

"What about your brother?" Noi turned back to Ghan, her voice growing more tense. "He . . ."

"He won't be able to lend us anything either," Ghan replied gently. "It's a bad year for the whole village."

"Then why did you bother asking me, Ghan? You knew there was nothing else to do but accept his terms."

Ghan touched his wife gently. "I wanted you to know too, that's all," he said. Then he jerked his head toward the fat man. "Satisfied?" he spat out in a voice full of rage and impotence. "Now go!"

"I'll go but don't forget, I'll be back next year," he said as he strutted off down the path.

Dawan's mother looked at Ghan. "You'll be owing him money for a long time to come."

"Don't you think I know that?" Ghan sighed heavily. "But there's nothing else we can do."

His wife shifted her baby to her other arm and started to walk slowly back to the house. "At least we don't have to live in the ugly, cruel City anymore," she murmured to herself.

When they had reseated themselves inside the dim, thatched home, Dawan edged closer to her cousin and asked in a small voice, "Noi, why did you say just now that the City is ugly and cruel?"

"Oh grow up, child!" Noi blurted out. "Everything is ugly and cruel. What kind of world do you think it is, anyway?"

"But, but before you told us stories of how perfect the City was," Dawan persisted, twining a strand of her hair round and round her finger.

"Well, that's all they were, stories! Little fairy tales!"

Reflecting Dawan's bewildered pain in her own eyes, Dawan's mother asked, "But why, Noi? Why did you tell us lies then?"

"What else could I have told you?" Noi retorted

angrily. "All you people wanted to hear about was some fairy tale about The Big City. Who was I to start telling you things you didn't want to hear and wouldn't have believed anyway?"

"And didn't you ever realize, Aunt," Ghan broke in gently, "when Noi used to prattle on about the fancy hotels and big factories, that a lot of men and women had to sweat to build and slave inside those buildings and factories?"

"I may never have left the village, Ghan, but I'm not stupid, you know!" Dawan's mother snapped. "I know buildings don't pop up like mushrooms, and that factories don't run by themselves." She paused, then asked more humbly, "But what is your point?"

"Well, the people who build the hotels never get to live in them, and the people who work all day in the factories never get to use the materials they produce. Don't you see, my Aunt? We are made to work extra hard and yet are paid less than we deserve, just so that businessmen might profit from our labor."

Dawan's mother sighed, tugging at the edge of her blouse. "Yes, I see, Ghan. After all, I have seen much the same things in the village too. Such a pattern of unfairness doesn't just happen in the City, you know. It is unfair, but," she glanced over to the thin frame of her daughter standing in the shadows, "but for Dawan, the City need not be an unfair place. She does not need to pay off any debt or work for anybody. She'll only go there to study quietly."

"That's what you think!" Noi blurted out. "Do you know what children from poor families usually do after school to feed themselves?" Her voice was low and sullen. "The younger ones carry little boxes of cigarettes and foreign candy around their necks, trying to sell some to people on the steps of movie theaters at night, people who either ignore them or swat at them as if the children were a pack of flies. Some of the more nimble ones dart between fuming cars at traffic lights, hawking newspapers. Or," Noi glanced over to her young cousin, and shrugged, "or, since Dawan is still fresh and sweet-looking she can squat in some side-alley where the police won't chase her away, and peddle faded jasmine garlands to the powdered women of drunken soldiers. Huh, and if she was a little older, my Aunt, worse things than this could happen to her." She seemed on the verge of saying something, but then decided against it. "I could tell you some things about the young girls in the City that would make your teeth fall out, my Aunt," she said bitterly.

"Huh, my teeth are not so loose yet that they would fall out from anything you youngsters have to tell me."

"I never told you, did I, how I was attracted to the dim dance houses when I first arrived? There were lights and music trailing from them at all hours of the night, and I was drawn to them like a moth to some candle flame. Thinking I could find a nice job in one of them, I walked into one late one night."

She paused, and held her baby a little closer to her. "Then I saw how brittle and ugly the women who worked there had become from offering whiskey and themselves to the swarms of white soldiers. I stumbled out of that place and sobbed in the streets for a long, long while." Her voice faltered, "And they were just healthy young women from villages like ours, good hardworking women."

Dawan asked, "The white soldiers, are they really as . . ." she hesitated, "as brutish and cruel as people say they are?"

Noi shrugged. "No more than any young men who're sent to live and fight far away from their own home would be, I suppose. They are rough, inconsiderate, but," she conceded reluctantly, "lonely too."

"It's not each soldier himself but the situation of having foreign soldiers on our land that is the real trouble," Ghan summarized.

"The City is made for the rich people and the foreigners, we villagers go there only to serve them." His wife paused meaningfully. "Including your daughter."

Listening to Noi's bitter words, Dawan felt a dread of the City for the first time.

"Yes, it's much healthier for a young girl to grow up in the countryside," Ghan was saying. "There is at least a semblance of equality and peace here. We still have our klongs, and monks and peasants, students and teachers, peddlers and shopkeepers, all riding up and down on the same klong-boats together. But in the City, rich people ride in big shiny cars, while the rest of us have to manage as best as we can walking around."

"Wait, what have boats and cars got to do with all this?" Dawan's mother asked warily.

Ghan tossed the hair back from his forehead. "Everything, if you had to spend all your waking hours filling up klongs to widen City roads!" he retorted. "I was part of a work crew, and had to unload truckloads of mud every day to fill up the little klongs that weave through the City. And what for?"

He looked around at the stubbornly quiet faces in the room, then punched his thigh angrily. "Why should I have to haul chunk after chunk of mud on my back in the fierce sunlight so the rich can lounge more comfortably in their air-conditioned cars. Is it right? Is it fair?"

Stirring uneasily, Dawan asked, "If things are so unfair in the City, how will remaining in our little village ever change anything?"

"Huh, have you ever tried to change anything in the City?" Noi answered sourly. "After a while, you get so discouraged that you'll learn to shrug it off and just live with things the way they are."

"I don't think I will ever learn just to shrug it off," Dawan objected. Noi muttered something under her breath, but her husband silenced her and told Dawan to go on. The young girl hesitated, then continued, "I mean, that's why I want so badly to go to school in the City. As it is now, all we ourselves know about are the little bits and pieces of unfairness that we have experienced. It's hard to change things, even the smallest thing, without changing the overall pattern that these things are a part of. I keep thinking that there must be a whole order to this, a system with rules and laws all mapped out in it. And I want to study how the system works and moves, and then I think I could help to find a better one."

Ghan looked impressed. "Where did you get these ideas, little cousin?" he asked her.

"Kwai and I have talked about it a lot," Dawan admitted shyly. "And our teacher always says that studying should be a way of learning how to help our people, and not just swallowing down and spewing up the words in textbooks." A twinkle flickered in Dawan's eyes. "Kwai always points that out to the teacher when he hasn't memorized or studied his lesson for the day," she added.

"Studying!" Noi humphed. "I've never been to school like you, so I don't know what sort of things you're counting on learning. All I know is that I couldn't change anything, that's all . . . No matter how hard I tried."

"But what did you try?" Dawan demanded, growing bolder.

"What did I try? I tried to get Ghan from being drafted. Then I tried to get a job in the City that would let me retain some self-respect, but I ended up as a white woman's servant-girl. Then I tried to see Ghan every once in a while, but the people I worked for wouldn't let him come near their compound.

"Why not?" Dawan broke in curiously.

The young woman shrugged. "How would I know? I think it was because Ghan's clothes were always torn and muddy from work, and she might have looked down on that. But then who really knows what is in the minds of those mango-red foreigners anyway?"

Dawan blinked. "Mango-red?" she repeated softly. "I thought they were white."

For the first time since their visit, Noi's laugh was loud and cheerful. "Originally they *are* white, a sort of stale bean-curd white. But as soon as they come into this country, they take off nearly all their clothes . . ."

"Even the women?" Dawan asked incredulously.

"Especially the women!" Noi replied with relish. "Then they sprawl under the blazing sun every day until they turn a funny red color, like overripe mangoes."

Dawan giggled, and even her mother's eyes went round in wonder.

"Tell them about their snakeskins," Ghan prompted, enjoying his aunt's reaction.

"Oh, and they *peel*," Noi continued. "When their skin turns red, it starts to peel off their arms and stomachs and even noses. Just like a snake shedding its skin!"

Dawan mulled over this, then asked rather timidly, "Was she pretty, your mistress?"

"She was not 'my mistress'!" Noi snapped. "I

mopped her floors and washed her clothes, and she gave me some money every month, but she was not 'my mistress'. Please get that clear."

There was a strained silence, then Noi continued more evenly, "Pretty? Well, she wasn't bad-looking, at least after she peeled. She always looked well, kind of shiny. She had lots of glittering clothes and strings of sparkling stones.

"She was not pretty," Ghan broke in firmly. "No one who lounges around all day ordering others to wait on her can be really beautiful."

"Ghan believes that true beauty is born from a person's own strength," his wife explained, a soft light shining from her eyes.

"Noi was seven months with child then, and still having to scrub floors and wash clothes. She was strong," he lowered his voice with dignity, "and beautiful."

Just then the baby woke up and started whimpering. Noi shoved her breast carefully into his little mouth, and it quieted down to suckle again. Ghan watched his wife and child silently, protectively. And seeing the three of them together like this in their shady hut, Dawan suddenly understood why they had returned to their village, and had hated the City, the crowded, ugly, heartless City.

Dawan's mother also sensed the closeness binding this little family. She whispered, so as not to disturb the baby, "It is time we leave. I understand much better now why you have returned to live in the village. But," she paused, then asked Noi awkwardly, "I suppose there's no chance, since you feel this way about City life that you would help Dawan convince her father she should go to study there?"

Noi shook her head, and turned to address Dawan directly, "It's not that I don't want to help you, Cousin. I just think that going to the City will do you more harm than good in the long run, that's all. It's my honest opinion, Dawan."

Ghan glanced over to Dawan and observed quietly, "I don't know if our opinions have any effects on Dawan herself. Look at her, she still wants to go, doesn't she?"

Dawan had knelt up as Noi was speaking, and was examining the gaudy postcards again. In one of them she had seen a few uniformed students, swinging book-bags from their shoulders—the pride, the power, and the promise of newly-learned knowledge in their laughter. Now she turned away guiltily and stared down at the smooth floor boards. "I want to see for myself," she said. And her voice was soft, but firm.

Chapter 5

The last streaks of sunlight were already slithering under the trees when Dawan and her mother started walking home. In the twilight lull, Dawan suddenly heard the light slapping of quick footsteps on the sandy path behind them. She glanced back and saw a nimble figure darting after them. "Mother, I think that's Kwai trying to catch up with us. Let's wait."

Dawan's mother glanced at the deepening shadows around her and shook her head. "I'd better be getting back to start dinner, child. You can wait for your brother if you want, just be sure to come back in time to gather some vegetables for me. We're out of cabbage already."

Dawan nodded obediently, and stepped aside to wait for her brother. Soon he came panting up to her,

his buffalo moving slowly ahead of him, and without a word of greeting, demanded to know where she had been. Dawan resented his abruptness, and said curtly, "What's it to you?"

Looking sharply at his sister, Kwai said accusingly, "You went to Cousin Noi's, didn't you? You dragged mother to see Cousin Noi to get her on your side, didn't you?" He paused briefly, scowling. "Well, is Noi coming over tonight to talk Father into letting you go to the City? What did Ghan say? Is he going to support you too?"

"Huh! If I knew you were going to be this impatient and rude, I wouldn't have waited for you!" Dawan retorted, quickening her pace.

Kwai hesitated for a moment, and then slapped the sides of his buffalo until the beast lurched heavily forward. "All right, sister, all right. I'm sorry," he said when he had caught up with her. "I was just anxious to know what happened."

"You sure were!" Dawan muttered. But, being as quick to forgive as she was to take offense, Dawan relented and told him, in bits and pieces, the gist of the discussion that had taken place in Noi's home.

When she finished, Kwai seemed stunned into silence. "You mean they don't want you to go?" he finally murmured, shaking his head in wonder. "And I thought they loved and admired the City so much! Huh!"

"That's what we all thought. I guess that's why Grandmother made me go over there. Now it'll be harder than ever to get Father's permission."

"You still want to go, then?" Kwai asked quickly.

"Oh, Kwai," Dawan blurted out in exasperation, "of course I still want to go. You should know that! You wanted to go so badly yourself. Just because you didn't get the first prize doesn't mean nobody else can go. I mean . . ." She stopped abruptly as her brother kicked his buffalo viciously. "What's the matter?"

"I may get to go yet," he growled.

A streak of fear shot through Dawan's heart. "What do you mean, Kwai?" Perhaps there had been a mistake, and she hadn't really won? Perhaps girls were not allowed to go after all? Perhaps . . . "What do you *mean*, Kwai?"

The silence that followed seemed interminable to Dawan. Finally her brother said, his voice slow and guarded, "I went back to school this afternoon, to ask the teacher how I had done. I just wanted to know, that's all, how badly I might have done, how much behind you I stood. For all I knew, I might have been at the very bottom of the class."

"Oh, Kwai," his sister muttered.

"You don't have to 'Oh, Kwai' me," he said curtly. "The teacher wouldn't tell me at first, said it was probably better that I didn't know. But I was stubborn . . "

"You always are," Dawan said under her breath.

". . . and I kept pestering him until he gave up and told me."

There was a dramatic pause. "Well? How did you do?" Dawan asked tersely.

For answer, Kwai snatched a big leaf from an over-hanging branch and tore it neatly down the middle. Tossing one half of the leaf away, he announced grimly, "I was second. Right after my own dear big sister."

"Does . . . does that mean you get to go instead of me?" she asked softly. Her heart was pounding.

Her brother looked her straight in the eye. "It means that if you don't go, I get to go." He tossed the other half of the leaf away and added, "Sister."

Turning away, Dawan drew a deep breath, trying to steady the beating of her own pulse. "I'm going, Kwai," she said firmly. "I'm sorry, but I'm going."

She looked up at him appealingly, and continued, "How can I give up my one chance? You know Father has already said that this will be the last year he will pay for my school-fee. If I don't use this scholarship I won't be able to get any more schooling. But you'll have many more chances yet. He said he'll send you to school as long as you want to go on studying."

"You mean he'll send me to school as long as he can afford to," Kwai corrected her bitterly. "High school, away in the City, is too expensive for him. He wanted me to get that scholarship so I could go on my own."

"But you could continue to study here, in the village school. Maybe next year you'll win the prize," Dawan argued urgently.

"The prize, the prize!" Kwai interrupted, mimicking his sister, "stop talking of the scholarship as a prize! It's not a victory, don't you see? You didn't win it!"

"What do you mean?" Dawan asked warily. "Of course I won it, I placed first, didn't I?"

"You didn't *win* it!" Kwai shouted in exasperation. "It's a responsibility, don't you see? This chance for further study just means that you have to be more responsible for helping those who didn't get the same chance."

Relieved that her brother was challenging only her concept of the scholarship and not her right to it, Dawan calmed down. "Look, Kwai, we've talked about all that before. Teacher said it just this morning. I know what you mean. I know what the importance of education is. I'll learn what will be helpful in creating change for our village, and . . ."

"It's fine for you to spout off ideals like that," her brother interrupted rudely, his voice growing louder and sharper at every sentence. "But what can you do to bring them about? You're only a girl. You won't be able to fight, or to argue loudly, or to lead people in times of crisis. All you're good at is study-ing—that's how you got the scholarship in the first place."

Dawan's hands were clenched so tightly that they were shaking. "Shut up!" She felt like screaming. "I'm every bit as good as you are! Shut up!" But she only said coldly, "And you think you can take on these responsibilities? You can fight and argue and lead, and help make a better place for the rest of us to live in?"

68

Kwai struck his chest with his hand. "Yes, I can!" he claimed brashly.

Dawan stood stock-still and glared up at her brother. "Well, so can I, little brother," she said acidly.

They continued the next few steps in stony silence. The singing of the crickets seemed shriller than usual, and grated on Dawan's nerves. "So it has really come to this," she thought with her first tinge of bitterness, "it's either him or me."

As if sensing her thoughts, Kwai suddenly said, "There's no way we could both go, is there, Sis? Take turns or something?"

"Oh Kwai, if only there were," Dawan answered, glad that their silence was broken. She grinned. "Can't you just see the confusion in the City teacher's face, if I showed up in class one week, and you in the next week?" Their gentle laughter softened the shrill cry of the crickets, and the hostility between them melted away. "If only we both could . . ." Dawan repeated, and sighed.

As they neared home, Dawan looked at her brother hesitantly, "Are you . . . are you going to tell Father?"

"Tell him what? That I came in second, right after you?"

Dawan could only nod and the fear in her revealed itself even in that slight movement of her head.

"I don't know, Sis. I don't know what to do anymore. If I tell Father, he won't let you go, and you'll probably hate me forever. And if I don't tell him, I'll never get to go, and end up hating myself."

They were approaching the last stretch before home now, and Kwai said heavily, "I guess I won't tell him, at least until I think it out some more."

Dawan's heart fluttered: there was still hope then. "Promise?" she asked urgently, as they turned around the bend and neared the house. Their father was stooped underneath the house, mending the chicken coop again. "You promise, Kwai?"

"I don't have to promise anything, Sister," Kwai retorted, and sprinted ahead of her to greet his father.

Chapter 6

Dinner that night was a tense and silent meal. Even the two smaller children sensed the uneasiness within the family, and refrained from their usual teasing and giggling. Dawan noticed with silent gratitude that her mother had added some fishballs in the vegetable soup, probably in the hope that this treat would soften her husband's mood.

However, when she tried to bring up the subject of her daughter's schooling, Dawan's mother was immediately silenced by him. "What is all this talk of Dawan going away to study?" he snapped. "It's too early to even consider it. Let it wait for a few days."

"But if I'm really going, I should leave within the week," Dawan protested.

Her father glared at her, "I *said*, let it wait!" he growled.

It was not until the end of the meal, as Dawan rose to collect the dirty dishes, that she mustered up enough courage to ask her father why he would be against letting her accept her scholarship.

He shoved a last spoonful of rice into his mouth, squinting savagely at Dawan. He was not used to being challenged for his actions. "Haven't you had enough schooling already? What do you want to keep studying for anyway?"

Dawan bit her lip and silently gathered the remaining dishes. As she walked away to the corner of the room that was the kitchen, she couldn't help but notice the soft smile on Kwai's face. She tried to catch his eyes, but he was nervously drumming his fingers on the floor boards, and did not look up at her.

"If I had won the scholarship, would you have let me go away to school, Father?" he asked abruptly.

"You?" his father spat out. "You didn't win anything. What's the sense of thinking about that now?"

"But if I had, Father?" Kwai persisted.

Dawan shot her brother a pleading look, dreading what he might say next. Kwai caught her look but lowered his head deliberately, to ignore her.

"If you'd won, of course it'd be different," the father answered. "You're a boy, and more schooling would have been useful for you." He paused, then added wistfully, "And useful for me too. Why, you could come back and help me to . . ." Then he shook his head, as if to clear old dreams away, "What's the sense of thinking about that now?" he sighed.

Kwai continued to drum the floor restlessly, still refusing to look at his sister. But he remained silent and went out of the house.

As soon as she had finished washing the dishes, Dawan dashed outside to find Kwai. But he had gone off on his own again and was nowhere to be seen. Feeling extremely restless, Dawan wandered down to the river.

In the velvet-warm sky, the first few stars had begun to glimmer, flicking some of their glow onto the river water below. For the first time that day, Dawan had a chance to ponder alone the question of studying in the City. She began to wonder if it was right for her to assert herself, to stand in Kwai's way. Perhaps her father was right after all; with more schooling, Kwai could find good jobs, and earn some money to help the family. Maybe some day he might even become strong and important, and have the power to change the injustices in their village and in the country.

And Dawan herself? What could she do? She was just a girl. Wouldn't she grow up just to be a wife and a mother? What could she do with more learning?

Nothing, the stars whispered coldly. Everything! their reflections in the river answered defiantly.

Dawan felt a strong need to struggle for her rights but knew this new will and determination would count for very little, without some outside source of support. Her father would not listen to her arguments; Noi, out of conviction, and her mother, out of fear, had refused to act on her behalf. And now even her brother was threatening to speak out against her for himself. To whom could she turn to seek help?

Just then she heard a soft splash in the river off to her left. She caught a glimpse of loose robes and gentle movements: it was a monk bathing by himself in the moonlit shadows. There was a sense of calm detachment, almost of unreality, about him. As a monk, and in the moonlight, he seemed apart from the everyday world.

As Dawan turned away, she suddenly smiled to herself. She decided to go to the temple the next morning, and talk to the head monk there. She knew that if there was one person in the village her father respected deeply, it was the gentle old monk of the village temple.

"He is a kind old man," Dawan thought, "and if I explain my difficulty perhaps he will help me. He might even come by our house some morning when he's out gathering food, and talk to Father about it face to face." A cool breeze brushed by, whispering something in Dawan's ear. She sucked her breath in sharply, "And if that happens, why then, I'll really be able to go away to study in the City!"

Chapter 7

In the gentle light of dawn, the marketplace looked very busy and crowded. Peddlers with their fruits, cakes, fish, cucumbers or straw brooms squatted on the muddy ground, keeping an alert eye on their wares. People of all ages and types mingled around, bargaining for flowers, munching on some fruit, carrying sleepy babies on their hips. Off in a corner of the market, a few monks threaded their way silently through the crowd, their orange robes fluttering in the soft breeze. Each cradled a bronze alms bowl in his arms. Every few steps they stopped to receive ladles of steaming white rice from the early worshippers who wanted to make merit by offering food to them. Dawan stood on the edge of the crowd hesitantly. She had never been to a market by herself before, since her mother or grandmother had always accompanied her on the special festival days when she had begged to go.

She looked around to see if anyone had noticed her uneasiness but they all seemed to be engrossed in their own affairs, counting coins and rearranging their wares. A plump woman hurried by, the gauzy fishtail in her rattan basket brushing against Dawan's arm as she passed. She glanced back at Dawan and smiled apologetically, then wobbled on.

Reassured, Dawan looked around for a flower stall, and saw a dark fat man perched rather precariously on a wooden stool guarding his buckets of flowers. Dawan approached him timidly and took a deep breath. "I would like to buy a lotus bud," she said in a small voice. The fat man was peeling a hard-boiled egg with intense concentration, and without looking up, he replied gruffly, "Twenty pennies."

Dawan only had the ten pennies that her father gave her once a week. She thought of buying half a flower, but doubted if the fat man would even put down his hard-boiled egg to consider it. Then she remembered that her mother always bargained heatedly before she bought anything at the market, and so she said, "Ten pennies." But her voice sounded hopeful rather than demanding.

The fat man only grunted and took a careful nibble at his egg. Dawan waited for a moment, and then asked, "You don't want ten pennies for your lotus flower?"

This time the fat man stared up at her from his stool and growled: "Look, child, I don't bargain for one silly lotus bud. Twenty pennies, take it or leave it!"

Since she could not afford it, she was about to walk away when she heard a girlish voice call from behind her. "Wait, you can have one of my lotus buds!"

Dawan turned around, and saw a young girl squatting on the ground. She was surrounded by sparrows in dainty wooden cages, and a white bucket full of lotus buds. The girl was smiling at her. Bending down eagerly, Dawan chose the freshest lotus in the bucket and lifted it up. "Can I have this one for ten pennies?" she asked.

"Sure," the girl replied cheerfully. "I pick these from the klong myself every morning, so they don't cost me anything." She caught Dawan's surprised look and laughed, "I go swimming in the river before anyone is awake. That's when I pick them." Lowering her voice, she confided with a wink, "But don't tell anybody!"

Dawan giggled and whispered back to the flower-girl that she sometimes went swimming secretly too, but thought that she was the only girl in the whole village that dared do it.

"Here," the girl said with a sudden burst of friend-liness, "why don't you take the flower free. It's a present."

"Oh no, I couldn't do that! It wouldn't be fair. See, here is my ten pennies." Dawan tried to hand

her the coin but was gently slapped on the wrist by the other girl.

"Keep your money. I got the flowers free anyway. They're not really mine."

"Well if they're not yours, how come you're selling them then?" Dawan challenged.

"My mother makes me," the flowergirl said sourly. "She and Father said that since I refuse to help inside the house, I'd better help outside of it. I used to hate having to spend all my time around the baby and the cooking and the washing, so I'd sneak away and explore the marketplace. Now that I have to be here every single day," she looked around her and shrugged, "it just doesn't seem that exciting anymore."

Dawan looked uncertainly at the girl and then at the coin in her palm. "Why don't you take it anyway," she offered. "You picked the lotus, didn't you?"

"Sure I picked it, but I didn't *make* it, did I? The mud held its roots, the water gave it life and the sun made it beautiful. Why don't you go throw your coin to the river or bury it in the mud if you really feel like you have to pay something?" There was a touch of defiance in the girl's twinkling eyes that Dawan both respected and liked.

"Well, thank you . . . thank you very much." She smiled, wanting to offer something in return. She suddenly decided that she would share the secret of her mission with this new-found friend. "I'm going to the temple with this lotus, you see. I'm going to try and see the head monk today," Dawan confided.

"Really?" The other girl lifted her eyebrows curiously. "It must be pretty important if you want to see the *head* monk!"

"Oh it is! It's the most important thing that can happen to me," Dawan whispered fervently.

"What can be so important to girls our age, Sister?" the flowergirl retorted.

"It's about my schooling," Dawan explained hesitantly, ignoring her last remarks.

"Your schooling, huh? You go to classes?" There was a grudging curiosity in the girl's voice. "What's it like anyway, learning . . . books and stuff?"

Dawan started to answer with enthusiasm, telling her of the storybooks they read, of the new ideas explained to them, of the sums they could do, but then she suddenly faltered and stopped. The flowergirl was listening to her so intently, a frank longing in her eyes.

"My brother goes to school, too," she muttered, mashing a stray feather into the mud beneath her big toe, "but he doesn't talk about it the way you do."

In the uneasy pause that followed Dawan avoided looking at the other girl's face. "Well, what does he say about school, then?" she finally asked.

The girl shrugged. "Vichai? Huh, he hardly even talks about it at all. He just . . ."

"Vichai?" Dawan interrupted. "He's in my class. He sits behind me." She looked at her friend with fresh interest. "So you're his sister? Funny, I never knew he even had a sister."

"Why should you? He never mentions me to anyone." She snorted, "Nobody ever mentions me. I don't go to school or do anything important. No, I'm just me, old Bao. I sell lotus buds and caged sparrows every morning, that's all. Nothing special ab . . ." She stopped abruptly, as if she had just remembered something. Leaning forward, she asked Dawan tersely, "Wait a minute, did you say you sat in front of my brother?"

"Well, yes I do—why?"

"Right in front of him?"

Dawan nodded. "Yes," she repeated warily. "Why?"

But Bao only remained silent, staring at Dawan's lotus. "Of course," she murmured after a while. "That's why it was so important . . . going to the temple today . . . and the head monk too . . ."

"What are you talking about?" Dawan demanded, flicking a fly off her ankle.

For answer, Bao looked the schoolgirl straight in the eye and announced triumphantly, "You're Dawan, aren't you? You're the one who won the school prize." Without waiting for any confirmation, she reached out and brushed aside the hair on Dawan's forehead and scrutinized the exposed forehead.

"You must have an awful lot of brains stored up in there to have won that prize," she commented.

Dawan pulled away, embarrassed. "Don't be silly, Bao. I'm not a freak or anything. Don't treat me like one!"

Bao withdrew her arm awkwardly and let it dangle

83

by her side again. "I didn't mean it in a bad way," she protested, a bit hurt. "It's just that, well, you do need to use a lot of brains, don't you, to learn to read and write and all the rest of it?"

Thoughtfully Dawan stroked her own cheek with the tip of the lotus bud. "It's not that people are born smarter or dumber than one another," she pointed out hesitantly. "It's the way different chances have been given or denied people that makes them so different after a while. I can read now only because I was given a chance to, when my brother helped talk our father into letting me study years ago and . . ."

"Waaa! I wish my brother would do something like that for me!" Bao exclaimed, sounding impressed. "All my brother ever cares about is himself, and most of the time he'll end up fighting me too just to get what he wants."

Dawan grunted. "Maybe all brothers are like that in the long run," she said slowly. "Even my brother is becoming like that now." Dawan told Bao of how Kwai had placed second on the exam, and was probably going to tell their father about it soon, so that she'd be forbidden to go study and be forced to stand aside for him instead.

Bao listened wide-eyed and indignant, and when Dawan finished, she demanded, "Well, what are you going to do about it? You're not going to just sit around there, and accept all this, are you?"

Dawan lifted up her lotus flower and waved it in

front of Bao's face. "What do you think I'm going to see the head monk for, silly!" she retorted.

"Oh I forgot," Bao answered, but she still looked dubious. "But you know monks," she began slowly, "they're not supposed to get involved in the affairs of lay people. That old monk is a kind and harmless fellow," she mulled, stroking a caged sparrow with her fingertips. "But I bet he won't take sides with you and go help persuade your father."

She eyed Dawan's single lotus bud critically. "Are you going to the Temple with just that one flower?" she asked.

"Why, do . . . do you think it's too little?" Dawan stammered, her fist wrapped tightly around her one coin. "I . . . I don't have much money."

"How much have you got? Enough to free one of these poor cooped-up sparrows? It's good to make more merit before going into the wat, you know. And besides," her fingertips caressed the sparrow's breast lightly, "these little birds are just dying to be free to soar back into the sky."

Dawan watched the bright, darting eyes of the caged birds, and she said eagerly, "I'd love to free them all!" She laughed at her own extravagance, then asked shyly, "How much would it be to free just one? I've got ten pennies."

Bao snorted, "Still that silly ten pennies of yours?" She stroked the feathers of one of the birds regretfully. "That won't be enough to free even half a bird."

85

Dawan looked at the coin in her palm and sighed, wishing that she could have made more merit before seeing the head monk.

"If I let you free one of them now, maybe you could pay me tomorrow," Bao suggested helpfully.

Shaking her head, Dawan gathered up her sarong. "I won't be getting any more money for a week. Well, I'd better get going." She stood up, then asked, "You'll be here later this afternoon, won't you? I want to tell you how it turned out with the monk."

Bao grimaced. "Sure, I'll be here this afternoon, and tomorrow afternoon—every afternoon for the rest of my life, probably!" She picked up the lotus bud that Dawan had chosen and extended it to her. "Here, you forgot this. You shouldn't go inside the Temple with empty hands, Sister."

Dawan reached for the flower, and the long stem was cool and slender in her fist. "Thank you," she said again to Bao.

"For what? The sunshine, the mud, the river water?" She laughed cheerfully, "You're welcome."

Chapter 8

To Dawan, entering the temple compound from the bustle of the marketplace was a small shock, like suddenly stepping out of a slashing thunderstorm into the shelter of a snug hut. As always, a carefully cultivated peace hung in the still air.

The stone slabs of the courtyard, polished smooth by countless bare feet, were warm under Dawan's feet. At the doorway to the temple itself, she wiped the loose dirt off her feet and straightened her blouse and sarong.

It was dark and hollow inside. The thinly fragrant smell of incense filtered through the cool dome. Two rows of monks sat near the altar in solemn stillness, chanting the Buddhist scriptures read in a deep voice by the head abbot, who was seated on a dais. On the floor space between the entrance and the altar a few village people sat quietly, their legs folded underneath them, like resting deer.

Dawan slipped unobtrusively to the front. With the lotus between her palms, she bowed slightly to the statue of the Buddha, and then carefully placed the bud in a big urn already half-filled with fresh flowers.

Creeping back, she sat down gently, tucking her sarong under her, and listened to the chanting.

When the head abbot had finished reading the scripture, the monks rose swiftly and, like airy orange moths, dispersed through the back door, into the old monastery.

The elderly abbot stood up more slowly, rearranging the folds of his robes about him. He was about to follow the other monks when Dawan realized that this was her one chance to approach him. She sprang up quickly and darted after him, ignoring the disapproving stares of the other villagers in the temple.

Her sudden movement caught the eye of the old monk, and he stood aside, watching her weave her way to him. When she reached the dais, she looked up, and saw even in the dim light that he had been waiting for her. He looked thin but strong, like a straight old pine tree in the twilight.

"Sir, can I see you for . . ." she started to ask him when she suddenly remembered that he was headed for breakfast. For a long moment she stared up at him, then whispered awkwardly, "I'll wait for you out in the courtyard, after you have eaten, sir," then she darted back past the other worshippers and disappeared to the back of the temple.

As always, the sounds around her were softly harmonious, suggestive of music rather than musical. Passing breezes tickled a row of temple bells on the eaves, making the two little ones at the end laugh lightly.

Once she stepped out from the dim gloom of the temple and into the open courtyard outside, Dawan felt more relaxed and at ease. Flocks of doves pecked at the crumbs that the monks had scattered on the grass, and a few old dogs dozed in the dappled shadows underneath Bodhi trees.

Dawan sat down on a stone bench and started whistling softly. Like many girls she knew, she could whistle with ease, but was too shy to do it when others were around. A few birds fluttered by, chirping, and others peered out curiously from behind a sun-splattered foliage. Pretending that she was singing a birdsong, Dawan's whistling grew louder and more spirited.

As she whistled, Dawan realized that there was no one else around. Usually the courtyard was dotted with quiet students, heads bent over worn schoolbooks. But school was over now, and nobody needed to retreat to the sanctuary of the temple grounds to read anymore.

Dawan's lively whistling now seemed hollow and sad to her, a mockery of the silent garden. The deserted benches glared at her, as if telling her that a phase of her life was over, and that she had no right to sit there anymore. She stopped whistling, and sighed softly.

"Why so cheerful one moment, and so gloomy the next?" a gentle voice murmured behind her. Dawan swung round and faced the old monk, whose smile was half-hidden in the leafy shadows beneath the tree.

Standing up hurriedly, the young girl could only mumble something about changing moods and how deserted the temple courtyard was now.

"It may be quiet now," the monk said quietly, "but in just a few months' time, there will be a whole new batch of earnest faces studying here again." He paused, and his eyes seemed a bit faraway.

"Well," the monk said slowly, padding his way across the grass with Dawan tagging after him, "You didn't come here just to walk with me, did you?"

The schoolgirl shook her head, and frowned slightly because she didn't know where to begin.

"It must be something quite important," the head monk prompted her. "You even brought a lotus for the altar this morning."

"I was going to do even more than that, sir," Dawan offered eagerly. "There were some caged birds in the marketplace, and I really wanted to free one to make merit." She hesitated, and added lamely, "Except I didn't have enough money."

The monk brushed aside her apology with a wave of his hand.

"But the birds looked so forlorn, all caged up like that," Dawan persisted. "They craned their necks to look at the sky between the bars of their cages."

Looking at Dawan, the monk said shrewdly, "You didn't really care about making merit, did you, child? You just wanted to see those sparrows fly away free."

"I, I guess so," Dawan admitted hesitantly, not sure if she should feel guilty about this or not. In the pause that followed, she added defensively, "After all, birds were meant to fly far and wide; they were meant to be free."

The old monk sighed, "All you youngsters are alike, talking of flying away and being free," he said, and his voice sounded a bit tired. "And where do you want to fly off to?"

"The City school," Dawan blurted out.

The monk stopped walking and stared down at the young schoolgirl. "Where?" he asked sharply.

"The City school, sir," Dawan repeated eagerly, walking ahead with steps as quick and as disjointed as her rush of words. "I never thought of flying off before, sir. But you see, I have this chance to go away to study now, only my brother wants to go too, but it was really me who . . ." Dawan flushed.

The head monk was frowning, cocking his head to one side to peer down at the nervous girl.

"You see," Dawan began again, "I, at school I, I . . ."

"Yes, I think I do see," the old monk interrupted calmly, leaning forward to look at Dawan with a

fresh interest. "You must be Dawan, the girl who won the scholarship. And your brother Kwai rather unfortunately came in second." He glanced at her with frank curiosity. "You two must be excellent students."

Her mouth dropped open, and Dawan looked at the abbot with awe. How did he know all this? Was it really true that great monks knew everything? "How, how . . ." she stuttered awkwardly, and then lapsed into silence again, not daring to ask him.

The thin old monk watched her with amusement. "You forget that your teacher and I are good friends. He told me about you two yesterday. If your cage door is already open, child, you're free to fly to the faraway City school. So what is troubling you? Is something keeping you back?"

Dawan nodded. "My brother, sir," she said reluctantly, feeling somehow that she was betraying Kwai. "He's blocking my way."

The monk raised an eyebrow quizzically, and Dawan hurried on to explain that if Kwai told their father he had come in second, as he had threatened to do, she would simply be ordered to step aside for her brother.

The old monk still looked slightly puzzled when she had finished explaining. "But what do you want me to do?" he asked.

"You, you could talk to my father, sir," Dawan replied eagerly. "He'd do what you tell him to—he respects you a lot, really he does. He'll listen to what you say, sir."

"And what am I supposed to say?" the monk asked wryly.

For a moment Dawan thought he was joking, because the answer seemed so obvious to her. But when she saw that the monk was really waiting for an answer she stammered, "Why, just say what's true, sir. Tell him I won first place and it is my right to go."

"Your right?" the monk murmured uncertainly. "But, but you're . . ."

Dawan tensed. For a second she thought he was going to say, "But you're a girl," and refuse to listen to her anymore.

But the old monk's sentence trailed off, and instead he quickly asked another. "But why do you want to go, anyway?"

"Why? Because I want to learn. I want to know everything! In the City school I can learn everything!"

"Everything you need to know is right here," the monk said calmly.

"In this tiny village?"

"In this tiny temple," he replied. "What can be more important than learning Buddha's noble truths, learning to accept the transience of life, to work towards achieving enlightenment, to . . ."

"I don't mean that kind of learning," Dawan interrupted, brushing back a stray wisp of hair from her eyes impatiently. "I mean learning things that would be of use to people, that . . ."

"Is Buddhism of no use to anybody?" the old monk asked coldly.

Dawan sucked in her breath and hung her head: she knew she had offended the abbot with her unthinking protests. Not daring to look up at him, she faltered, "I, I didn't mean that, sir." Her voice was low and hesitant, "I just meant that I wanted to know how to cure sick people, or to help set up a new order where farmers would own their own land —we have to pay so much rent now, sir—or . . ."

"You have a good heart, child," the monk said, more gently now. "But Buddha saw the sufferings of the people too, you know. We call him the Compassionate One, remember? He saw old age, and sickness, and death, and he was disturbed by what he saw just as you probably are now."

He paused to see if Dawan was listening, and then continued, "But he realized only after a long search that no-one can stop suffering; one has to go beyond it."

"How do you go beyond suffering?" Dawan asked, trying to keep the wariness out of her voice for fear of offending the old monk again.

"You learn to stop wanting things, child. First you realize that nothing that we touch, or see or hear or smell or feel will last forever. Things we perceive will only pass away after a while. Flowers fade, parents die, the sun sets." He glanced at the young girl quickly. "Can you understand that?" he asked.

Dawan nodded, a bit dubiously.

"Well then, once you realize that things of this world don't last, then you also see that they are not really important. So you learn to stop wanting ordinary things, and are able to concentrate on the higher truths. You . . ."

"Wait, if ordinary things aren't important, what *is* then?"

"I was getting to that. You know what Nirvana is, don't you?"

"It's when you reach enlightenment, like Buddha, and don't get reborn again," Dawan rattled off, as if repeating some formula which she had memorized without having understood its meaning.

The abbot nodded approvingly, "When a man reaches Nirvana, he is freed from the wheel of life, of being born, of suffering, of dying and of being born all over again. In Nirvana there is no suffering, no pain, no rebirth, only nothing."

"No happiness or joy either?" the schoolgirl asked.

"That's the point, child. What's the sense of being happy? In the end you only lose the thing that makes you happy anyway. Nothing lasts forever, you know."

"Nobody was talking about it lasting forever, sir," Dawan protested. "But what is wrong with just trying to make it last a little longer?"

The old monk smiled, but in his eyes there was a lingering sadness. "A little longer?" he said and sighed. "What for, child? What's the sense of going through life always dreading the end of some fragile happiness?"

They had reached a small pond where the turtles lived, and both stood silently beside it, watching the small black beaks of the turtles nibbling at the layer of duckweed on top of the still water.

"But when I'm happy, I don't want it to end," the schoolgirl persisted, dropping a small pebble into the pool and watching the ripples radiate outwards.

"Of course you don't, child. I didn't either, but that was a long time ago. Now I know that everything must end, and I accept it. I don't clutch on to things anymore." The monk's voice was hushed and gentle, like the sound of receding waves on the seashore. "Life is calmer and less painful this way, believe me."

Seeing the frown on the young girl's face, the monk shook his head slightly and smiled. "But you don't believe me, do you?"

"If I am happy, I want to hold on to it as long as I can, that's all. It's only natural," the young girl repeated stubbornly.

"But if you know it will have to end sooner or later," the monk argued, a bit exasperated now, "why bother to hold on? Why try to clutch onto a passing shadow, child?" He looked at the reflection of a cloud sailing across the small pond.

"That's easy for you to ask," Dawan argued bitterly, "you live inside a peaceful monastery, and have your food and clothes provided you, and nobody dares bully you. You don't have to live with the pain that we do in the world outside the temple."

"Be careful what you say, child," the abbot warned

her sternly. "You are still young, and do not fully understand the wisdom of those who have lived five times longer than you."

"I don't have to be wise to know that someone who's suffering doesn't just accept it," Dawan retorted heatedly. "People learn to struggle, to fight against the pain in life."

"But what for? In the long run, what for?" the monk demanded. "Can't you understand that we all die in the end, whether it is at seven or seventy? People live their whole lives pretending they won't die, taking everything as seriously as if they will live forever. Don't you realize that even if you help a little now, or manage to change things to a small extent, none of this will last?"

"It doesn't have to *last!*" Dawan cried. "As long as there's *some* improvement in things, even if it's only for awhile, it's a worthwhile effort."

"So many have tried to improve things, child, but . . ."

"But I still want to try!" Dawan interrupted earnestly, her eyes gleaming. "Even if you've tried, and failed, even if thousands of thousands before you have tried and failed, I want my chance to try too!"

"You will just be wasting your time and spirit," the old monk maintained, a deep frown hovering above his eyebrows.

Dawan took a deep breath. "Does, does that mean you won't help me, sir?"

"Help you? You mean talk your father into letting you go to the City school?"

The schoolgirl could only nod stiffly.

Like a tired breeze through dry weeds, the old monk sighed softly. "How can I help you do something that I don't believe in? You're still young, child, but I don't think you should waste any more time dreaming such futile dreams. What can a mere schoolgirl hope to achieve anyway? Be satisfied with what . . ."

But Dawan was not listening anymore. "A mere schoolgirl?" she repeated sharply. "So it's come to that again, has it? You're just like the others after all. You won't help me because you think I'm a girl and unable to . . ."

"Child, be still," the monk interrupted, a tinge of anger in his voice. "That is not the reason."

Dawan shook her head vehemently, "It is the reason, it is! If my brother came and asked you to help him accept the scholarship, you would do it for him, wouldn't you?" she accused angrily.

"He wouldn't need to," the monk answered. "If he had gotten first place in the examination, there would have been no problem to begin . . ."

But Dawan had already swung around and was now running awkwardly away. At the gate of the temple courtyard, she turned back to glare at him one last time, her eyes squinting from bitterness as much as from the sun.

The old, thin monk stood still, watching her, and for one brief moment a glint of sunlight on his smoothly shaven skull seemed to catch and reflect the shiny tears from the young girl's face.

Chapter 9

Stumbling past the temple gates, Dawan tried to blink back her angry tears. Once outside, her fierce anger dissipated, leaving only a sense of quiet futility in its wake. She walked slowly and each step that she took was as heavy as her heart.

What, after all, was the sense of trying so hard, of hoping and arguing, if in the end the only result would be more frustration? If Kwai were the one going to study in the City, things would never be this difficult for him: should she just graciously give in to him now then?

Dawan suddenly felt very small and very tired. She leaned against a nearby tree, resting her forehead on its rough bark.

From the edge of the marketplace, Bao spotted Dawan slumped against the old tree.

Springing up from her stool, Bao threaded her way through the baskets of pickled mangoes and red peppers until she stood directly behind Dawan. Laying a hand on her friend's shoulder, she murmured, "Come, it couldn't have been as bad as that!"

Startled by the touch, Dawan swivelled around and faced Bao. They stared at each other for a moment, then Dawan turned away again, shrugging Bao's hand off her shoulder.

Undaunted, the flowergirl edged over to the other side of the tree, until she stood facing Dawan again. "Please tell me," she said, this time in a gentler tone.

Without lifting her head, Dawan began brokenly, "I couldn't . . . he wouldn't . . ." her voice trailed off. She spread out her hands in defeat, and cried softly, "Oh, what's the use?"

Bao snatched up one of those outstretched hands and, clucking sympathetically, led her friend back to her flower-stall.

"Here, sit down and tell me about it," Bao said, pointing to her stool, and squatted down herself.

Dawan sat down obediently but did not answer. Instead, she stared glumly at the pail of lotus buds in front of her.

"Well, what happened?" Bao repeated.

"Well, what do you think happened?" she snapped.

Bao eyed her friend warily, unsure whether to press her for more details or not. Finally she said in a soothing voice, "The old monk isn't that important anyhow. What are you going to try next?"

"What *can* I try?" Dawan moaned. Still staring at the lotuses, she sighed once, deeply. "Nothing," she said in a flat voice. "Nobody can help me, or would want to."

Bao snorted. "Huh! If you start believing that, then it will come true." She clenched one hand and continued, "But if you *don't* believe it, why, then you can try on your own and . . ."

"And then it needn't be true!" Dawan finished eagerly, as if a spark of hope had been rekindled in her.

Bao nodded excitedly. Taking a deep breath, she blurted out, "We girls have always had to stand aside and let our brothers do all the challenging things. And when we become wives, we'll have to stand aside for our husbands. And when we're mothers, we'll stand aside for our children." She jabbed Dawan with her finger. "You've earned your chance for flying to a bigger world, to pursue your own ideals. Don't yield to your brother now. You have to push forward and struggle if you want to be free, and equal to your brother."

Leaning over suddenly, she picked up the caged sparrow that Dawan had been quietly watching and thrust it at Dawan. "Here," she said eagerly, "open the door to its cage. Go on! Open it, you'll see what I mean."

Dawan set the cage down, looked briefly at Bao for a final confirmation, and then carefully pulled open the little door to the wooden cage.

The sparrow inside watched Dawan's movement with unblinking eyes, but made no move to fly out. Instead, it hopped timidly over to the other side, studied the open door again with cocked head, and remained still.

Bao slipped her finger between the bars and prodded the bird gently. It hopped over to the open door, fluttered out of the cage, and looked up, down, left, right, front and back.

Finally it seemed to realize that it was free. And then, with a single-minded grace, it soared off into the cloudless blue sky so swiftly that Dawan could hardly keep her eyes on it.

Dawan craned her neck to watch it wing away until it was just a tiny speck in the distance. Only then did she look back towards Bao, and say breathlessly, "I see what it is you mean."

Bao acknowledged this with a brief nod, and added thoughtfully, "For you, the door may not even be open that long. You must dart out quickly and fly free with your own set of wings! Just like that tiny sparrow!"

Dawan reached out and pressed her friend's arm warmly. "Thank you for showing me . . ."

Then she felt Bao's arm stiffen. Bao was no longer listening. Instead, her attention seemed riveted onto a figure striding towards them from behind a nearby fish stall.

"Quick! Hide!" Bao ordered urgently, her voice low with dread.

"But what for? Who are you afraid of?" Dawan whispered.

Bao pointed quickly to the approaching figure. "It's my brother. The bird . . . you can't pay, can you? He'll be furious!" She shoved Dawan away roughly. "Hurry! Run!"

"But what about you?"

Bao waved the question aside. "I can handle him, I think. Now hurry up and go!"

Looking back uncertainly, Dawan darted away. When she came to a stall hung heavy with woven baskets, she stopped abruptly and hid behind it. Then she peered out and watched Bao's stall.

Bao's brother swaggered up to the stall, his eyes sweeping over the pails of flowers and bird-cages in quick calculation. Then he said casually, "All right, Sister, how many birds did you free this morning?" His voice was smooth and sly, and sent shivers down Dawan's spine.

"You can see for yourself, Vichai," Bao answered calmly. "There are four empty cages."

"You know I didn't mean that." His tone was still smooth, but had grown low now, with hints of thunder in it. "How many birds did you free without collecting money for them, Sister?"

"None."

"You little liar! Why are there four empty cages and only seventy-five pennies in the box?" He stepped towards her menacingly.

Bao spread out an arm protectively over her birds,

"All right, all right. I freed one," she admitted sullenly. "I won't do it again."

"That's what you always say, you brat," her brother growled. "Then two days later, you'll let another of these stupid things fly off again."

"I said I won't do it again!" Bao said, more impatiently. "Now go away and mind your own business."

"This *is* my business!" Vichai shouted. "I caught those birds and put them in the cages. The whole thing belongs to me. And if I ever catch you short of money again, Sister . . ."

"Those birds don't belong to you or to anybody else." Her eyes flashing, Bao had scrambled up and now stood confronting her brother. "And you just wait, someday when you aren't spying on me, I'm going to set the whole bunch of them free, you hear!"

From behind her screen of baskets, Dawan saw Vichai raise his left hand, but before she could shout a warning, he had delivered a stinging slap across Bao's cheek.

Bao did not flinch. Squinting fiercely at him, she stuck her chin out and taunted, "Aren't you a brave strong one? Hit me, why don't you hit me again, you money-making bully!"

Vichai clenched his fist, but before he had a chance to strike her again, Bao ducked down and opened as many cage-doors as she could. With a sudden flurry, small brown shapes darted out, fluttering and

chirping excitedly. With her hand lightly shielding her hurt cheek Bao watched the scattering flight of the sparrows with a grim glee.

Vichai also watched for a split second. Then he brought his fist down again, hitting Bao sharply on the shoulder. She screamed, but continued to yank open the little cage-doors as if her life depended on it.

Dawan could not bear just to watch anymore. She rushed out from behind the basket stall to help her friend. At that moment, she caught a glimpse of her own brother dash over to Bao from the opposite direction. Before she could reach them, Kwai had grabbed Vichai's arms and was struggling with him, trying to keep his flailing legs from hitting Bao again.

Among the pile of broken birdcages, Bao sat crumpled up and silent, oblivious to the scuffle before her. As if in a world of her own, she was gently holding a brown, feathery shape in her cupped hands.

As Dawan stepped closer, she saw that it was a dead sparrow. "Oh Bao, Bao," she whispered, kneeling down beside her new friend.

Bao looked up from the small bird, and her eyes were cool and clear. "It's dead," she said tonelessly, her voice more tired than sad. "It's dead now. I killed it. I crushed it."

"But it wasn't your fault," Dawan pointed out gently. "He pushed you down on it."

But Bao was not listening. She turned the little sparrow over in her hand, trying awkwardly to put its broken neck back in joint. "See, it's dead. It won't ever fly back into the sky again. It's dead."

There was a strange stillness to her movements as she got up slowly, her hands cupping the small sparrow.

Both boys were panting, but Vichai had calmed down, and was staring sullenly at his sister. Bao stepped towards him, the sparrow balanced carefully in her outstretched hand.

"Well, are you satisfied now, Brother? Do you still want to sell this little bird? You could sell it for a discount, you know."

The anger that smoldered in Vichai's eyes seemed for an instant to catch fire again as he swung out to slap his sister. But Kwai immediately restrained him. Vichai thought better of it, and let his palm fall loosely to his side instead. Then, wriggling free of Kwai's hold, he strode away, pushing his way through the crowd.

Bao turned back to Kwai, and thanked him quietly for helping her. Then, with more curiosity, she asked him, "Haven't I seen you somewhere before? You look familiar? Do I know you?"

Kwai shook his head. "My name is Kwai."

Bao frowned. "Kwai?" Then she understood, and looked down at Dawan, who was still kneeling next to the broken bird-cages. "Your brother? This is your brother Kwai?"

In the tense silence surrounding them, Dawan found that she could not speak. She nodded cautiously, watching Bao, then turned back to face Kwai. The tears that the flowergirl had been too proud to shed over the dead sparrow now came streaming forth.

"Another brother! What false help I've been given! Kwai, Kwai, why do you help other people's sisters, when you are so mean to your own?"

Kwai stared at her, startled and confused. "What are you talking about?" he asked.

"Who are you to pretend to help me?" Bao demanded, her voice rising. "You're just as mean as my own brother, and even more sneaky. Pretending to help others when you're bullying your own sister! Inside you're just another bully, bully!"

"What do you mean?" Kwai too was getting excited and angry. "I don't know what you're gabbling about!"

"You don't know huh? Ask your sister! Ask her who's been trying to grab her chance to finish school! Ask her who's been working things so she doesn't get to go! Go on, ask her!" Bao shouted, glaring at him, her tears a jagged streak on her face.

"You little busy-body! Who told you this? How dare . . ." He raised his fist and, like Vichai before him, seemed about to strike her.

Dawan jumped up and tried to grab her brother's arm, shouting, "Don't you hit her too! Don't!"

But Kwai twisted away and growled, "Let go! You keep out of this!" With his other arm, he pushed her roughly aside. Dawan, who had been leaning forward, was knocked backward, and thrown off balance. With a startled cry, she fell right on top of the pile of broken bird-cages.

A piece of splintered wood sliced through her ankle, and Dawan felt a hot searing pain ripping through her left leg. She looked down, and saw that blood was streaming out from the cut around the ankle.

As if in a daze, she lifted her head up and stared at Kwai. Shaking her head from side to side, she murmured, "My own brother, my own brother."

Kwai had, in the meanwhile, bent down beside his sister and was clumsily trying to wipe away some of the blood with a part of a smooth banana leaf. But at his touch, Dawan jerked her leg away. Ignoring the crowd of people gathered around peering at them, she started screaming at Kwai. "You liar!" she shouted, her voice sharp but broken, "You're just a bully after all. Go ahead, use your strength, knock down the people who get in your way!"

Stunned by the outburst, Kwai remained completely still, his fingers slightly stained with his sister's blood, held stiffly away from him. He kept staring at Dawan, but did not seem to really see her.

"Why, Kwai? Why did you talk and talk to me of helping poor people and weak people, and then turn around and try to grab from me the one chance that was meant for me? Why did you make me believe in you, if all you really are is a big bully? Did you mean to fool me, Kwai? Did you? Or is it because something in your ideals has already gone sour?" She bent down to peer at her ankle again, and as each drop of blood trickled out and splashed delicately down into a mud-puddle by her feet, she chanted softly, "Liar, liar, liar . . ."

The crowd listened to all this with a hungry silence. Then, from among its fringes came a loud voice demanding to be let through. There was a jostling from one section, and the people parted slightly to let a disheveled young woman into the middle of the ring.

It was Noi, panting slightly and carrying a half-filled basket of vegetables from the crook of her arm. She knelt down hastily beside Dawan, and without a word, whipped out a clean scarf and started wiping her cousin's wound.

"Somebody give me a bucket of fresh water," she ordered in a business-like tone. And seconds later, a bucket was carefully handed over to her. As she gently washed Dawan's ankle, the crowd realized that the excitement was over and slowly drifted away.

Dawan did not seem to notice either the dispersion of the crowd nor Noi's careful nursing. She closed her eyes and felt a limpness permeate her, as if all her vitality and feelings had been drained away.

"These people!" Noi was muttering under her breath as she washed and wiped Dawan's cut, "Always standing around gaping when someone gets hurt, but never offering any help! The useless . . ." She stopped short as Dawan jerked her ankle away. "Does it hurt, child?" she asked in a milder tone.

Dawan nodded, but did not open her eyes. Noi looked at her and asked suddenly, "How did this happen, anyway? Who hurt you like this? How did it begin?"

Dawan pursed her lips and remained stubbornly silent.

"Was it Kwai?"

"Yes! Yes it was! He pushed her down. It wasn't her fault at all!" Bao, the only one left of the crowd, squatted down to join them. Without bothering to introduce herself, she launched into the story with gusto.

Noi listened to her with some amusement, and a certain wry sadness. By the time Bao had finally finished, Noi was already bandaging her cousin's ankle with an old handkerchief. She patted Dawan's shoulder lightly and said, "You see what happens when you try to have your own way, Dawan? In the long run it's not worth it to fight with boys. You've only got a cut leg now, but next time it may not be your own brother you're fighting with, and you may be hurt even more. Believe me, it's painful in this world to get in the way of men."

For the first time since her cousin came to help her, Dawan lifted her head and spoke. Her voice sounded faint but urgent, like the cry of a bird lost in the night, "But, but you don't understand. We're friends . . . he wouldn't hurt me . . ."

"What do you mean he wouldn't hurt you!" Bao snorted. "What do you think he just did?"

Even as she was listening to Bao, Dawan felt a

few drops of wetness splash onto her arm. She blinked in surprise: she didn't think she was crying—whose tears were these then?

Somewhere off in the distance, she heard the faint growls of the sky-belly. Tilting her head upwards, she saw that lumpy rainclouds were gathering directly overhead. The sky was beginning to look like a raggedly plowed field.

Noi and Bao had both risen and were tugging at her to stand up. Elsewhere, the villagers were scurrying around the marketplace, packing up their piles of vegetables and cakes. Children darted about, searching for shelter under the remaining stalls as the fall of raindrops quickened. A gust of wet wind snatched at Dawan's sarong as she struggled to stand up, leaning on her cousin's arm.

"Here, you take my umbrella," Bao shouted, above the din of the marketplace and another roll of thunder. As she stooped down to pick up her faded orange umbrella, she noticed the dead bird, its feathers damp and ruffled by the rain, lying on the ground. With one hand she grabbed the umbrella, and more gently, with the other she picked up the sparrow.

"Poor thing, I won't have time to bury you after all," she said to the sparrow cupped in her palm. Handing the umbrella to Dawan, she looked around for a shelter for her bird. Off in the corner of the opposite stall was a little pile of wilted flowers and torn leaves. Bao walked over to it, and laid the sparrow on top of the leaves. Then she placed a few fresh lotus pads from her own bucket on top of the bird. When she came back to Dawan she was smiling thinly. "I always thought birds needed umbrellas too," she explained.

Noi had gathered all her things together now and, with a final order to Dawan to hurry home before the storm hit, rushed off. Dawan was left standing under the umbrella with Bao, still feeling a bit dazed.

"Is your ankle all right? Can you walk on it?" Bao was asking her. "I can walk you back to your house if you need."

"No, I can manage pretty well. It doesn't even hurt too much anymore. Thanks anyway."

Bao watched her friend limp off. Then she shrugged, and sprinted off in the other direction, towards her own home.

Chapter 10

Although her ankle ached each time she stepped on it, Dawan was grateful for the solitude afforded her by the walk home. Like the raindrops pattering on her umbrella, her thoughts beat down on the surface of her brain, lightly and urgently. The rain had grown steadily heavier, splashing on the wet path in front of her. If she didn't hurry, the fury of the monsoon storm would be upon her.

And yet Dawan dreaded the thought of returning home. She dragged her feet along as she imagined the sharp questioning she would have to face from her parents when they saw her cut ankle. Most of all, she shied away from the possibility of having to confront her brother again.

So, at the fork of the dirt road, instead of taking the path home, she turned right and headed for the river. Despite her ankle, she hurried along this path, feeling a mounting urgency to sit alone next to the quiet calmness of the river.

But the river was far from calm! As she approached its banks she saw the waters were swollen with rain, and its color had turned a sullen gray-green. Restless waves reared up and broke over the fragile riverside reeds. She glanced over to the old bridge to see if it would be safe for her to climb up on it and just sit awhile. But Kwai was already there.

Dawan's first impulse was to dart back to the leafy shelter of the path, before he could see her. Too much hurt and hatred had already been generated between them this morning, and she was afraid that confronting him now would only intensify the pain.

And yet, even as she backed away, she sensed that much more still needed to be said or the wide gap that separated them now might never be bridged again.

As she stood hesitating, a gust of wind slashed past her, nearly snatching her umbrella away. Dawan shivered, and then sneezed violently. It was getting chilly, and the storm would be just minutes away.

"That dumb brother of mine is going to catch a horrible cold, sitting out here like this," Dawan muttered to herself. Then, without thinking twice about it, she hobbled up to the foot of the bridge and called up to Kwai, her voice sounding thin and damp in the rain.

"Hey!" Dawan shouted, "You're going to catch a cold sitting out in the storm!"

Startled, Kwai jerked his head up and stared at her. Then his eyes slid down to Dawan's feet, where her bandaged ankle was poised gingerly on the ground, like the hurt paw of some puppy. As if roused from some deep sleep, he frowned, blinked hard, and then called down, "Does your ankle hurt?"

"Sure it hurts," Dawan said. Then she noticed her brother rubbing his big toes together in embarrassed shame, and she shrugged and added lightly, "But it'll heal soon."

An unspoken awkwardness hung between them.

Then, all at once they both spoke up. "What are you doing here anyway?" Dawan demanded, and the same second Kwai asked, "Why did you come here?"

They glared at each other warily, then finally both of them broke into a grin.

"What am I doing here? I'm sitting on top of the bridge thinking," Kwai answered lamely.

"Uh-huh, and I'm standing at the bottom of the bridge telling you to come down out of the rain," Dawan smiled.

"I'm not coming down."

"Why not?"

"I told you, I'm thinking."

"You can go home and think."

For answer, Kwai only shook his head, and bent down to stare at the water again.

"Well, what are you thinking about?" Dawan asked. And although she had wanted to make her voice sound stern, her curiosity came through clearly.

Kwai hesitated. "I don't know. I guess I was thinking about what happened just now, in the marketplace. And what you said to me." He paused, and there was a pained look on his face. "What you said, after I pushed you, it isn't really true, is it?"

"What? You mean about you being a bully?"

Kwai nodded, and rubbed his toes together fiercely, "And about how easily my ideals had soured."

Even though the wind and rain was building up, Dawan waited a long while before she replied. Finally she looked up at him and said slowly, "That's something only you can know, Kwai."

"But did you mean what you said, Sister?"

"I meant it then. But it may not be true. You hurt me and I was angry."

Kwai frowned, as if unsatisfied with the answer. "But what you said, it did make sense, you know. How can I say that I want to study more so I can help people later on, when the only way I can get this further schooling is by robbing my own sister of her chance to study?" He turned to look at Dawan, biting his lips. "It just isn't right, is it?"

"Of course it isn't. You would be saying one thing but doing another!" Dawan blurted out.

"Well, what should I do then?" Kwai asked tersely, his hands gripping the wooden boards.

"What should you do?" Dawan repeated incredulously. "I don't have the right to tell you what you should do, Kwai. It's something you'll have to think out for yourself."

"But I want to know what *you* think," Kwai persisted.

"You *know* what I think. But you still have to think it out for yourself."

Kwai nodded dubiously, and was about to answer when a big sneeze interrupted him. "I, I *have* been trying to think, Sister. That's what I was out here for, only . . ." Another sneeze, more violent than his first, cut his sentence short.

His sister looked up at him in exasperation. "How can you think when you keep sneezing every three seconds? Can't you at least come home and think in a dry place?"

"No," Kwai insisted stubbornly. "If I have to think this out by myself, I'm going to stay here to do it." He looked at her, and added by way of an explanation, "I think best by the river." Shoulders hunched against the rain, he gazed at the water and muttered, "Besides, some thoughts are worth catching a cold for."

In a vague way, Dawan could understand her brother's need to be in the midst of a thunderstorm while he was trying to make such a serious decision.

Dawan sighed. "Here," she said, thrusting the umbrella into Kwai's hand, "if you must think out in the rain, at least use an umbrella."

Without giving him time either to protest or to thank her, Dawan turned away quickly and climbed down the bridge again. She needn't have bothered to hurry, though. Sunk within his own conflicts as he was, Kwai did not even notice the umbrella in his hand

until Dawan had already reached the bottom of the bridge and was starting down the path home.

Only then did he catch a glimpse of his sister hobbling awkwardly into the tree-lined path, bare-headed and empty-handed. Startled, he glanced up and finally noticed the little orange roof above him.

By now his sister was already drenched with the rain, and only with painful difficulty could she hobble along, trying to keep her wounded ankle out of the many puddles on the road.

Kwai scrambled up, and rushed down the slippery old bridge, nearly tripping over the umbrella in his haste. "Wait!" he shouted above the sound of the wind and rain, "I don't want your dumb umbrella! You take it!"

Far away as she was, Dawan heard him, and turned her head to shout back, "You're going to be in the rain longer than me, stupid!" With that, she continued to trudge on, head bent against the slashing rain and arms wrapped tightly around her chest.

Under the shelter of the orange umbrella, Kwai stood stock-still, watching his sister limping down the narrow path. Just a few hours ago, he had hurt Dawan badly, but now she had left her umbrella for him to sit under in the rain, while she limped clumsily home, wet and cold and tired. Kwai suddenly knew his decision was made.

Holding the umbrella high above his head, as if he was flying a kite, he raced off nimbly after his sister, so that he could catch up with her and share the umbrella the rest of their way home.

Chapter 11

As Kwai came splashing noisily down the path, Dawan spun around and gasped, "Now what are you doing?"

"Me?" Kwai panted in wide-eyed innocence. "I'm going home, of course!" He slowed down his pace to walk beside his sister, holding the umbrella carefully over both of them.

Dawan looked at him warily, "But what about thinking things out on the bridge?"

"Out in the rain like that?" Kwai asked, mimicking his sister's tone just a while before. "Only a fool would sit out in the middle of a rainstorm to think." He looked at his sister, and shrugged. "Besides," he added airily, "I've got things all thought out anyway."

Dawan stopped in her tracks and stared at her brother. There was a long pause. Finally she said, "Well?" in a very small, very tight voice.

Try as he might, Kwai could not hold back his grin. "Well? Well, what do you think, Sister, what do you think?" he chanted mischievously and turned to walk on.

His sister stood rooted to the spot, clenching and unclenching both fists as if trying to grasp the real meaning behind her brother's words. Kwai had stopped and turned back to face her, and was now shouting, "Hurry up, dummy, I'm not going to offer you this umbrella twice, you know!"

Dawan understood then and broke out into a beautiful, broad grin. Half-hopping, half-dancing, she ran up to join her brother under the umbrella again.

The two children huddled together, protected from the slashing rain. Neither of them spoke, but a strong sense of trust bound them together in companionable silence.

At the fork of the path, Kwai suddenly stiffened and grabbed his sister's elbow, pointing to their left.

"What's the matt . . ." Dawan began, and then quickly broke off as she too saw the figures ahead of them at the junction of the road. Even in the mist and heavy rain, she could tell immediately that it was their father leading the buffalo home.

Perhaps it was the strange gloom of the storm, or perhaps something in the way the tall peasant stalked ahead, which made both Dawan and Kwai uneasy at once.

"Better let him go first," Dawan whispered to her brother, "maybe he won't see us."

They drew back into the wet shadows of the path, and watched tensely as their father approached. "He looks angry," Kwai murmured. "I wonder why?"

Dawan suddenly jabbed her brother in the ribs. "The buffalo, you idiot!" she exclaimed. "You're the one who's supposed to bring the buffalo out of the storm!"

"I completely forgot," Kwai groaned softly. Then, straightening up his shoulders, he added, "I'd better run up and offer to lead the dumb animal the rest of the way home."

His elder sister put out a restraining arm. "But he's going to be very angry with you, Kwai."

"Well, I've got to face him sooner or later, don't I?" Kwai argued. "It might as well be now."

Dawan hesitated, then, straightening her own shoulders, announced, "All right then, I'll come too."

Kwai flashed her a toothy smile. "We've only got the one umbrella between the two of us anyway, Sister."

They stepped out of the tree shadows and walked quickly, if a bit fearfully, until they had caught up with their father. Head bent against the wind, he did not hear them approach. Only after Kwai called out to him did he swivel around and glare at them.

"Well, *there* you are!" he snarled, and it seemed to Dawan that his teeth shone pale with a glint of raindrops.

"I'm . . . I'm sorry about the buffalo!" Kwai stammered. "I can take it the rest of . . ."

"Never mind the damn buffalo!" the father shouted, over the noise of the rain. "Why didn't you tell me about the exam results?"

Kwai's mouth dropped open. "The exam results?" he repeated dumbly.

"Don't pretend you don't know what I'm talking about, you rascal! You knew you placed second yesterday!"

Ignoring his father's question, Kwai asked in an awed whisper, "How, how did you know of this?"

"I just talked to your teacher," his father answered gruffly.

"But he wouldn't tell you . . ." Kwai protested.

"He thought I already knew," his father said impatiently. "He called me over to his schoolhouse this morning to ask which of you I had decided to send away for schooling." He paused, squinting his eyes a little, "The rest I made him tell me."

A fierce wave of thunder rolled by, and the two children huddled closer together under the umbrella. But their father seemed to draw strength from the sound, and stood even straighter and taller in the rain.

"Well," he demanded again, this time even more violently, "why didn't you tell me?"

"Because, because Dawan didn't want me to," Kwai stammered.

His father frowned, then turned and stared at the thin wet girl blankly, as if he didn't understand what she had to do with any of this.

"We, we had to di-discuss it between ourselves first,

Father," Dawan offered feebly. "We were afraid that you would . . ."

The lean peasant raised his palm threateningly. "Afraid, afraid! I'll give you something to be afraid of!"

Both children shrank back, cowering under the umbrella as if it was a shield, but his blow was a careless one, and only landed on the backside of the buffalo.

Startled by the sudden slap, the buffalo lumbered off into the forest bordering the path, dragging a wet tangle of vines and leaves in his trail.

Glaring at Kwai, their father jerked his head towards the buffalo, in a silent command for his son to pursue it. But Kwai stood by his sister, refusing to budge.

"Go!"

Kwai shook his head, his hands gripping the umbrella handle tightly. His father stared at him in disbelief. "What? Are you defying me too?" Kwai did not speak but quickly dropped his eyes.

The father turned his back on both of his children and stalked off after the buffalo himself, his strong bare legs kicking savagely through the puddles.

Kwai and Dawan watched as their father was swallowed up by the leafy web of the jungle. Then Dawan turned to her brother and asked, haltingly, "Are you sure now, Kwai? I am not forcing you to do this? What if you regret it later?"

Kwai hesitated, glancing at his sister's small face. Despite the orange glow that the umbrella cast on her,

Dawan looked drained and sallow. With her lips drawn in a taut line, and her eyes squinting against the wind, she looked as if she was bracing herself for a sudden slap. Kwai reached out impulsively and gently brushed a wisp of damp hair away from her cheek. "Yes, Sister," he answered solemnly, "I'm sure," and started to plod homewards again.

By the time they had reached the house, the rain had subsided, and only the sudden shuddering of leafy trees scattered some wayward raindrops down onto them. Dawan noticed their grandmother first, shivering slightly in her sleeveless shirt underneath the house. The old woman lifted up a bony arm and beckoned for the children to join her.

Dawan steered Kwai away from the steps and to the shelter under the house. From upstairs came the baby's broken sobbing, interspersed with soft cooing sounds from their mother. Their grandmother was shaking her head, but her eyes were more curious than disapproving.

"What did you two do to your father? He's in a fierce mood, he is!" she said in a conspiratorial whisper.

"Why, what did he do?" Kwai asked nervously.

"He came home shouting and cursing, then he stormed upstairs, throwing off his wet clothes and flinging them at your poor mother." The old woman glanced at Dawan shrewdly, "It's about your scholarship, isn't it?"

Dawan nodded, but before she had a chance to explain, a deep voice rumbled down, "Who's jabbering

down there? Are those two children here? I want to
see them *now!*"

His wife's head peeped out from behind the doorway, looking like a frightened pigeon. "Come up,
Kwai, Dawan." Her eyes were wide and unblinking,
her voice barely above a whisper. "Your father wants
to speak to you."

"Speak? I'll do more than *speak* to them!" came the
bellow from the darkness within the house.

Kwai reacted to the gruff voice as if he'd been
whipped. His brown face taut and determined, he
scampered up the ladder.

Dawan seemed reluctant to follow him, and instead gripped her grandmother's arm.

"I'm scared, Grandmama," she whispered urgently.
"I'm real scared inside."

The old woman grunted, and squeezed Dawan's
hand firmly. "Now don't you start being scared all
the time too, child! Your mother's bad enough . . .
let's not have two rabbits in the household! Besides,
what is there to be afraid of?"

She patted her own stomach proudly. "After all,
where do you suppose that big fierce man upstairs
came from?"

Dawan smiled wanly, and the old woman continued,
"And I daresay he was even more scared than you are
when *his* father got angry and started shouting. Why,
he was gentle and quiet once too, you know."

She paused, her eyes gazing out at the newly washed
fields, and added softly, almost to herself, "And if he

132

is tougher and louder now it is only because too many burdens have callused his skin, and worries have sharpened his voice."

Dawan hesitated, and gave the old woman a quick light hug. "All right, Grandmother, I'll be strong, and brave." She stepped up and climbed the first rung of the ladder.

There was a twinkle in the old lady's eyes as she looked up at her young granddaughter. "You certainly ought to, Dawan," she said and chuckled softly, "for aren't you the child of my child?"

During her brief delay in coming upstairs, Kwai had apparently managed to calm down his father somewhat, and they were now seated facing each other on the worn, smooth floorboards. They took no notice as she walked up to them and sat down silently next to her brother.

Their father sat cross-legged, a dry cloth draped across his bare shoulders. He spoke in a low monotone, deliberating over the choice of each word. "But you understood what it meant, to have come in second, didn't you?"

Without any hesitation, Kwai replied, "I understood, Father."

"And yet you didn't tell me of it."

"No Father, I did not."

"You deliberately kept it from me."

"Yes, Father."

"Why?"

"Because my sister wants to go study in . . ."

"Your sister, your sister! But I thought *you* want to go to the City School so badly yourself!"

"Yes, of course I do," Kwai sounded tired but patient. "But it is not my right to do so."

"But what right does your sister have? She's only a girl," the peasant retorted roughly.

With a sense of shock, Dawan realized that he was genuinely bewildered.

"She did best in our village," Kwai insisted calmly.

"But now?" the older man asked suddenly, his voice soft and guarded, like a cat on the prowl.

"Now, sir?"

"Now I know you placed second, even without your telling me."

"So?" Kwai asked warily.

The farmer paused. "What if I were to order you to go?"

"I will not go, sir."

"You still will not go, huh? But what if," his father stopped, and looked over to Dawan. "What if I will not let your sister go?"

"But she was the one who won the scholarship. You have no right to forbid her, sir," Kwai protested.

"I may not have the 'right', son," he grunted, his lips curling a little. "But I certainly have the power to do so."

Dawan said, "Even if you have this power, Father, you should not misuse it so."

Her father's eyes were like little bits of steel glinting on his dark face. "I wasn't talking to you," he growled.

"But I am talking to you, sir," Dawan replied evenly, her hands locked tight behind her back. "We've . . ."

"Don't you dare talk back to me, girl!" her father bellowed, "And stay out of this!"

"Why should I stay out of it?" Dawan challenged, her voice quivering from fear as much as from determination. "It concerns me too."

Father and daughter glared at each other, until Kwai cleared his throat and declared quietly, "If you don't let my sister go, Father, then Takchit will get to go."

"Who's Takchit?" he asked suspiciously.

"He's a very good student," Kwai answered coolly. "He was third in the exam."

The peasant's dark eyes darted from his son to his daughter in confusion, and then suddenly he seemed to understand. He grabbed Kwai's arm and yanked it hard. "You would give up your chance to go for somebody else?" His voice broke. "Just to spite me?"

Kwai's eyes were bright with defiance, but his answer was still calm and measured. "Not to spite you, Father, but to show you that I do not want my sister to give up her chance for me."

"You mean that?"

"Father, I mean it."

Looking slightly dazed, the farmer released his hold on Kwai. Then he turned and directed his next question at Dawan.

"And what have you to say, little daughter?"

Dawan looked her father straight in the eye. "Only

135

that I hope you will be as fair and kind towards me as my brother has been, Father," she said softly.

"Did you force your brother into taking this position, into letting you go?"

Dawan smiled faintly, "Can anyone 'force' my brother into anything?"

"Then why . . ." the father lapsed again into a bewildered silence.

"Father, I told you why," Kwai said in exasperation. "Because . . ."

"Let me hear from Dawan herself!"

Dawan hesitated, then retorted with a defiant, "Well, why not?"

"Why not!" the big farmer shouted at her. "Damn it, I'll tell you why not!" Dawan could see the veins on his neck as he shouted. "Because you're only a girl, because there's nothing you can do, even with a fancy education, because . . ."

"Father, stop it!" Dawan screamed in a hoarse voice, above the noise of the peasant's shouting.

"Father," she continued shakily, "if you keep thinking that I'll never be capable of doing anything worthwhile, then of course I really won't." She paused, struggling to find the words to explain herself. "Because I won't ever have a chance to, don't you see? It's like thinking a caged sparrow can't fly, and then refusing to open the cage door to give it a chance to even try."

The dark room remained submerged in tense silence, leaving Dawan's words floating in a little island of their own. Although the peasant's eyes were directed on his daughter, his gaze seemed to be on something untouchably faraway.

Taking a deep breath, Dawan continued with urgent sincerity. "There's a wide, wide world out there, Father, and so many things I want to learn and see and do. If you can share in your son's dreams why can't you share in mine too? Don't keep me caged in now, let me have my chance to fly out too!"

"So," he finally said, "so you want me to open your cage door, Dawan, and you think you'll soar off and do great things for us all, for the village, and the country, even the world?"

"I can try, Father," Dawan breathed, her heart pounding. "I can try."

The lean peasant stood up, flexing his knees carefully to uncramp his leg muscles. His two children scrambled up too, never taking their eyes off him.

Standing in a tight triangle, they exchanged glances silently. The tall peasant looked down at Dawan solemnly. "Then try, my daughter," he said. And he smiled, a bit reluctantly, down at her.

Dawan burst into a wide, wide smile and swivelled around, about to hug her brother. Only then did she catch sight of Kwai's face.

He was standing straight and proud, as if he too had won a victory. His jaw was set, and his eyes were bright and steady. Perhaps a bit too bright, Dawan realized, almost glistening.

Kwai lowered his head, turning away slightly so

that his face was hidden from her now. The exuberance that had welled up in Dawan seemed to choke suddenly in her throat, and she could find nothing to say to her brother.

Just then, a bright teardrop splashed near Kwai's foot. It glistened there for a second, and then was silently absorbed into the smooth floorboard, leaving only a small dark stain on the dry wood.

Why must it be this way, Dawan wanted to cry out. Must one person's joy be based on another's sorrow? Why must someone be left behind when another spurts ahead? Why can't we develop together, and move forward together?

She remained silent, staring only at the tear-stain at Kwai's foot. Even as she watched, Kwai inched his big toe slowly forward, until it reached, then gently covered, the little wet spot.

Chapter 12

Once again hints of morning drifted into the sleep-filled home. Dawan turned over in her mosquito net, listening to the sounds that she had grown up with and loved so well. The whispering of the weeds, the rhythmic moaning of the bull-frogs, the rustling of thick leaves in the jungle, and the song of the crickets had sifted through so many of this young girl's dreams that they seemed absorbed into her very being. Lying there, she listened to these night sounds seep away, until only the silence of dawn was left.

So this was to be her last morning at home. It seemed like all the other mornings that she had ever known, and yet there was a special glow somewhere, a lingering sadness in the cool dawn air.

Not wanting to wake the others, Dawan got up

quietly. With a few deft motions, she rolled up her rattan matting, and crawled out of the thin net. She glanced over towards Kwai's net, and out of habit almost whispered to him before she noticed that his bedding had also been rolled up and already tucked neatly away.

Dawan sighed. This was the most special of mornings to her, and she had wanted so much to share it with her brother. But Kwai had awakened and gone off without waiting for her.

Despite her deep disappointment, this did not surprise Dawan. Her brother had been sullen and moody for the past few days now, and had avoided her whenever she tried to approach him. It was not that he was just hostile and jealous of her—that she would have been able to understand. It was something more elusive and yet basic, a sort of gentle forlornness.

And now it was dawn, a dawn to be treasured. But she had no-one to share it with. Dawan braided her hair slowly, and then walked out onto the veranda and to the steps.

She climbed down the ladder, feeling a bit more light-hearted with each rung, until, as both feet touched the cool firm mud, she seemed quite spirited again. After all, she reasoned to herself, there is always enough joy and freshness in the early morning to wash away the heaviness clinging to your heart!

She darted down the rutted path to the river, catching quick glimpses of the lively patches of sun speckling the gloomy jungle leaves.

Stooping briefly to examine a dew-spun spider web balanced on three blades of grass, Dawan noticed that there were fresh footprints on the muddy path just in front of her.

They were just about the size of Kwai's!

Not quite daring to hope, she hurried the rest of the way to the river. And, once there, she looked immediately towards the river-bend.

Sure enough, on top of the old wooden bridge was her brother, squatting in the morning sun.

Dawan stood at the edge of the river and looked across to the fields that stretched out to touch the domed sky. The calmness of the fields seeped into her. Then she looked back at Kwai, perched on the bridge with the grace of a resting butterfly.

She could not believe that she was leaving in an hour, and yet she sensed that everything, the river, the fields, the bridge, even her brother, were all bidding her goodbye.

She walked over to the bridge, her feet knowing their own way. Kwai took no notice of her approach, but was completely absorbed in throwing pebbles into the river, sullenly watching each one as it hit the water and sank from sight.

When she reached the foot of the bridge, she called up to him, but he gave no sign of acknowledgment. "Kwai," she called again, "can I come up too?" Still he ignored her, and continued to throw his pebbles in, each one with more force and anger.

Finally he muttered to himself, "Stupid stones! All

they can do is sink, sink, sink to the bottom. No matter how hard you throw them, no matter how big a splash they make, all they do is sink." He threw another one in, and watched in disgust as it sank from sight. "And even their ripples fade away, and the water flows on, as if nothing ever happened. Stupid, stupid, stupid." He stopped abruptly and glared down at his sister, "I didn't get in your way after all, did I? Now are you satisfied?"

Dawan felt a sharp pain and pity shoot through her, and she wanted to run up to him and hold him, rock him clumsily like she did when they were both very little. Instead, she climbed up the bridge and sat down next to him, with the little pile of pebbles between them.

They maintained an uneasy silence, each staring directly ahead into the tendrils of the rising sun. Finally Dawan said gently, "Kwai, thank you. Thank you very much."

For answer, Kwai threw another pebble into the water. "Why do you have to go anyway?" he challenged. And although his voice was hostile, Dawan knew that, in his way, this was a plea too. Quietly, without looking up, she said to the ripples in the water, "You know why. We've just begun studying, and there's still so much more I need to learn, Kwai."

"Why go and study more when all you're going to end up doing sooner or later is cook and raise babies anyway, like Mama?" he demanded, punctuating every few words by hurling a pebble onto the smooth river surface.

"Well, why do *you* want to go study then?" she retorted angrily. She reached over for a pebble and flung one into the water herself. "All father's ever done with *his* life is plant some rice and raise chickens, and a buffalo or two. He's never gone to school, so why should you, when all you're going to be is just another peasant anyway?"

She grabbed another pebble from the pile, but her fingers touched something warm and bony: it was Kwai's hand reaching for his own pebble. They glared at each other for a split second, and then Dawan snatched her hand away.

"Kwai," Dawan continued in a softer tone, "I'm not even sure I really want to go to the City to study. You know how scared I am of crowded places. You're not helping me any with your angry questions, Kwai. Can't you see that I'm confused and scared too?"

She could feel the tears welling up from her lower eyelids as she spoke. All the things that had been pent up inside her for the past few days streamed forth as she continued, "Why can't you be happy for me, Kwai? I know it's hard, but if you had won the scholarship and were going instead of me, I would have been so happy for you, really, really I would have! Remember all the ideas you used to talk about? You dreamed of learning enough to help Father improve his crops, or to take the land away from the landlord and divide it among all the villagers, or to . . ."

"Well, I can't do any of that now, can I?" Kwai broke in bitterly, and although he still sounded angry, his voice was choked.

"But Kwai, don't you see? I can do all those things," Dawan continued eagerly. "All those mornings that we watched the sun rising, I listened to you talk of building a new world. I never said anything much because I never thought I'd have a chance to do anything. But I did listen and I believed in what you dreamed. And now that I've been given this chance to fulfill our ideals, you should be glad for me. Oh Kwai, everything will be better, I promise! I'll make things better!"

Kwai stared at his sister, whose face was shining with a new hope and strength. Then he lowered his gaze to his small pile of pebbles, and felt all the more lonely and deserted.

"Sure, things will be better," he blurted out. "Better for you! What am I supposed to do while you tromp off to a big fancy school in the City? Go sit with the dirty old buffalo all day and be glad for you? And in the early mornings, am I supposed to come out to this stupid old bridge and watch the stupid old sunrise and talk to myself?"

His voice broke, but he took a deep breath and went on more calmly, and yet with more urgency. "Nothing will ever be the same, Sister. I don't care if things will be better or worse, it's just that when . . . if you come back, we couldn't ever sit on the bridge and just watch the dawn like we used to anymore. You've changed that, you've gone and changed all that already." Almost automatically, Kwai's hand stretched out for a pebble, then stopped half-way in midair. "Oh, what's the use?" he said softly to himself.

In the silence that followed, he picked up a lotus bud lying on the other side of him, and began restlessly plucking off its petals.

Dawan noticed this, and because she hated to see fresh flowers destroyed, said sharply, "Stop that! Why are you tearing that lotus apart?" She was about to snatch it away from him when he shrugged, and tossed the bud aside.

"I liked watching the dawn with you too," she continued in a gentler, sad tone. "Can't you imagine how much I will miss that when I'm alone in the City? I won't have a chance to watch a quiet sunrise over river water anymore. Kwai, you know I'll keep wishing I could be back here on the bridge with you. I'll miss everything so much."

There was a pause, and then she said softly, "Hey, Kwai, when you're out here in the early mornings, will you watch the dawn for me too? And maybe you can sing my morning song for me, because it belongs here, and I'll never sing it anywhere else. Please, Kwai? Do you understand? Watch the dawn for me, and sing."

Her brother's face was now streaked with tears, cool, lonely tears which he didn't want his sister to see. Abruptly, without looking at her, he ran down the bridge and across to the fields, until he disappeared between the tall ricestalks. Dawan watched him run away, but this time made no move to follow him.

She picked up a pebble and dropped it into the

water, and as the ripples slowly quivered their way outwards, she started singing her morning song one last time:

> "Misty morning,
> mist is rising,
> melody of trees,
> slowly sifting . . ."

and as she sang, she let the hope of the morning light filter through her pores, until the delicate wonder of being home and leaving home blended together like sunlight through rainclouds in her heart. "How can I leave this?" she thought to herself, her song left unfinished. "How can I bear the loneliness in the big City, without friends, without Kwai, without the quiet dawns? I don't want to go off all alone and yet I have to. I don't, don't, want to but I have to, have to leave." It was as if these confused thoughts swirling inside her blurred over the morning scene itself with a misted film. Funny, she thought to herself, how the world looks like after-rain when I'm crying inside.

Then she noticed the half-torn lotus bud lying forlornly by her side, where Kwai had tossed it just now. Out of some feeling of kinship for it, Dawan reached over and picked it up, holding it with both hands, much the way she used to hold onto her grandmother's thumb when she was just learning to walk. Then she knelt up and carefully gathered the petals Kwai had stripped off and sprinkled them gently over the surface of the klong-water.

Like a fleet of tiny pink boats, the petals floated lazily down the water, rising and falling with each ripple of the river. Dawan watched them silently, then whispered, "See, see, Kwai, these don't sink. See, don't be sad, don't be sad, these don't sink." Then wiping away a stray tear, she got up and walked slowly down the bridge.

She knew that at home the bus would soon be arriving, and people would be waiting for her to leave.

Chapter 13

Peering out from the leafy shelter of the path, Dawan watched the crowd of villagers gathered around her home. Naked babies scurried between people's legs chasing chickens; a cluster of solemn young monks talked in low whispers among themselves; little girls peeped out from behind the curtain of their mother's sarongs.

Dawan caught glimpses of a few people who were special to her. Her teacher was standing rather awkwardly by himself, Bao was carelessly holding onto her baby brother while arguing with her older one. Noi was chattering and giggling with a knot of young wives while Ghan stood behind her sullenly.

Dawan stared at all this bustle for a moment, then hastily retreated into the shadows of the tree. But her mother, tying the last rope around her daughter's luggage, caught sight of the movement. She straightened up and hurried over to her daughter, shouting, "There you are! I was getting worried, child. Your father has already gone out to look for you. We thought you had suddenly decided not to go. It's a good thing you didn't run off for the day, child. Why, look at all the people here to see you off . . ."

By this time the villagers were swarming around, fussing and cooing over her. Dawan cringed back, muttered something about having to change her clothes, and wiggled her way through them. She clambered up the ladder to the hut, which she knew would be empty except for her old grandmother.

In the dim light of the house, Dawan saw a pair of steady eyes gleaming in the corner. "Don't be afraid child. Calm down," her grandmother said gently. "I have put your new clothes and shoes on the matting there. Are they all waiting for you outside?" She clucked softly, "Never *mind*, child, take your time."

Dawan smiled gratefully at her grandmother, and walked over to the piece of matting where her new things lay waiting. As she bent down to put her shoes on, she realized that she was still clutching Kwai's discarded lotus bud in her hand. Tossing the bud aside, she dressed hurriedly, her nervousness increasing as she heard the sound of the heavy old bus rumbling in. Outside, the noise of the crowd grew, like palm fronds rustling in the wind before a monsoon storm.

"Child, you come here."

Dawan obediently crawled to the corner where her grandmother sat, and knelt down in front of the old woman, hands neatly folded and head bowed. This was the leavetaking that pained her most.

In a voice slow and heavy with age, the old woman said, "You have a long life ahead of you yet, child, and this is just the first step. If you're this timid now how on earth are you going to face all the struggle still before you? Gather yourself together, and face the world out there with clear bold eyes. You hear me?"

Dawan nodded, but did not budge. It was the rhythm more than the meaning of the aged voice that calmed the young girl.

Her grandmother gave her a gentle shove, "Well, child, you must go now. You've packed everything you want to take with you, haven't you?"

Dawan stared at her blankly, then shook her head. "No, no, I can't go yet!" she blurted out. Swallowing hard, she continued desperately, "Please Grandmama, I'm not ready. I haven't packed everything yet. There's the sunrise I want to take, and the bridge over the river-bend. And, oh Grandma, how can I pack Kwai, and home here, and the chickens, even the bullfrogs in the forest, and . . ." She could feel a sob rising from her throat, but could not stop it.

Already it seemed as if these precious drops of childhood were slipping through her fingers, like sun-sparkles when she washed her hands in the river. Dawan glanced down at her one outstretched hand, and it looked so small, so helplessly empty. She wept then, shoulders hunched over as sob after sob was wrenched from her thin frame.

The old woman reached out and cupped her granddaughter's ears with feeble hands, but Dawan only shook them off.

"Let me cry, Grandmama," she sobbed brokenly. "Let me cry now and I promise, I won't ever cry anymore. Oh, let me cry now!"

So the grandmother withdrew her hands, and waited patiently until Dawan's sobs began to subside.

After a while the gentle old woman got up and hobbled, back-bent, to the rain-barrel. There, she picked up a small glass jar and scooped some fresh rainwater into it. Walking back to where the lotus bud lay on the matting, she bent over and put it carefully in the jar.

Dawan wiped away her tears with the back of her hand, and watched curiously. There was a solemnity about her grandmother's movements that suggested a sacred ritual, like the sprinkling of holy water over a newly-wed couple.

It was not until the old woman had unhurriedly reseated herself beside Dawan, that she handed the glass jar to her granddaughter.

"Hold on to this lotus carefully, child," the grandmother said. "Watch it unfold during your long bus-ride to the City. It's like yourself, this lotus bud, all shut up tight, small and afraid of the outside. But with good water and strong sunlight, it'll unfold, petal by petal by petal. And you will too, Dawan, you will unfold too."

"But, but I don't want to," the schoolgirl mumbled. "I don't want to change."

"I'm sure that bud you have there is pretty contented the way it is," the old woman smiled, nodding towards the lotus. "But if it refuses to change, it'll never become a lotus in full bloom, will it?"

Dawan shook her head reluctantly.

"And remember, the lotus shrinks back into a bud when night falls, only to unfold again in the dawn. Just because you're leaving now doesn't mean you'll never come back. And when you come back, of course some things will change. Anybody can see there's always change. What people seem to forget is that there is a beautiful pattern to all this change."

"But I'm not afraid I won't ever come back, Grandma," Dawan protested weakly. "Right now I don't know if I even want to leave in the first place."

"Don't think of this as leaving, then," the old woman answered firmly. "Think of it as just another of your petals unfolding. For me, child, life has always been an endless unfolding: night unfolding into day, girls unfolding into women, women unfolding babies from themselves. Why, life itself unfolds to death, and death unfolds to life again. There is no cause for sorrow or for fear in this."

Then, as Dawan still hesitated, her grandmother gave her another light push and said, "Go now, child."

Dawan looked at the lotus bud uncertainly. The glass jar was smooth and cool in her hands; somehow it seemed able to absorb the anxiety within her. She swept her eyes over the familiar walls of her home.

Sunlight and laughter stole in through the windows and hopped about on the wooden floorboards. Dawan took a deep breath, and nodded. She was ready now.

Setting the jar aside, Dawan pressed her palms together and bent her head over them to her grandmother in the traditional gesture of leave-taking. Then she stood up and, lotus-jar in hand, went outside to the veranda. Her mother and some other women were busy loading her luggage onto the already crowded bus, trying to wedge the bags between a big basket full of bananas and a coop full of squawking chickens. Everybody was fluttering about excitedly trying to help.

As she climbed down the stairs, her father rushed out from the jungle path, panting and scowling fiercely. He caught sight of Dawan at once, and strode up to her.

"Why did you disappear like that just before you're supposed to leave?" he yelled at her angrily. "Do you know that I've been chasing around the countryside the whole morning looking for you and Kwai? I thought the two of you had taken off together, until I saw Kwai alone. Where the hell have you been anyway?"

Ignoring his last question, Dawan asked eagerly, "Where is Kwai, Father? Where did you see him? Is he coming?"

Her father snorted loudly. "Huh! That brother of yours! And I thought the two of you were such good friends!"

"But where is he, Father? Is he coming?" Dawan

craned her neck to peer behind her father, but no-one was in sight.

"Where is he? He's sitting out on the old bridge, calm as a water-buffalo, that's where he is. I asked him where you were, and he said he didn't know and didn't care. Then I asked if he was coming back to see you off. He . . ." The strong peasant paused and eyed his daughter shrewdly, "You two had a fight, didn't you?"

Dawan did not seem to have heard the question. "Is he coming or not, Father? What did he say?" she asked tersely.

"You really want to know what he said? He looked down at me from his bridge and said, 'She's got the whole village seeing her off. Isn't that enough? What does she need me there for?' And I thought you two were . . ."

Dawan turned away so that her father could not see her face. She felt more lonely on the fringe of that chattering crowd than she had ever felt before. Looking at all the faces around her, she realized that there was not a single one she really cared to say goodbye to.

So her brother was still bitter and angry at her. She wondered again if fighting with him to go to the City had been worth it after all. She was leaving, but there was nothing left to say goodbye to.

The bus honked sharply, and Dawan saw the bus-driver wave impatiently for her to board. Immediately the crowd surged over to her, and she was shoved, patted, hugged and somehow pushed to the steps of the bus. She caught a glimpse of her mother crying, but she herself felt no more sadness, only a throbbing disappointment.

As soon as she got on, the big bus ground to a start and roared off. She groped her way clumsily to a seat and leaned out the window to watch the crowd. Her grandmother was standing on the veranda above them all, smiling slightly. Then the faces all receded into the distance. When they had disappeared from view, green stretches of paddy-fields slid past her window, going by as quickly as slippery fish. Ahead of them now was the river, and Dawan stuck her head way out of the window to catch a last glimpse of the bridge on which she had so often greeted the sun.

Suddenly, carried by the breeze, she heard a very familiar voice singing a very familiar song—

"Misty morning,
mist is lifting,
melody of trees
slowly sifting . . ."

He was there. Etched sharply against the cloudless sky, Kwai was standing on the old arched bridge, both arms thrown back in a gesture meant both to embrace her and to send her off.

Dawan burst out laughing and the laughter was so strong and round that it seemed to jam in her throat. Flinging her arms out too, to hug him and the land, she joined him in song.

"Dappled morning,
sun is flying
breaths of breezes
rising, dying,
brushing over the earth's brown skin . . ."

The bus was fast approaching the slim figure now. A grin, a streak of wetness gleaming on one cheek, an out-stretched palm, and Kwai had already flashed past her.

Leaning out as far as she could, Dawan watched her brother wave until he was only a speck on the bridge, until the bridge was only a speck on the river, and until finally even the ribbon of water faded into the distance.

Dawan watched for a moment longer, and then, gently picking up the glass jar from her seat, she leaned back. The morning song was still in her. So, brushing the lotus bud with her fingertips, she sang the last verse.

"Happy morning
my heart is singing
arms spread wide,
the dawn is bringing
its sunglow to this land, my home."

And as she sang, a shaft of sunlight pierced through the grimy bus windows and cradled the lotus. Dawan noticed that the first few petals of the flower had already begun to unfold.

Like most stories, *Sing to the Dawn* is partly true and partly a dream.

There are girls like Dawan in the villages of Asia who hope to study in the city and return to help their people achieve a better life. That much is true. But not many of these girls have this opportunity. For most of them, a scholarship is only a dream.

In a beautiful way this story may make the dreams of many Thai girls come true. All the money we earned in writing and illustrating the book will be used to establish scholarships for young Thai girls from the countryside.

That is not much, we know—but it is a start. If you could support us by sending a contribution to the fund we have started, you could help us make this dream come true.

For further details of the scholarship, or if you wish to make a contribution, please write to:

> The Dawn Scholarship
> A/C No. 3873-9
> Thai Farmers Bank, Head Office
> Silom Road
> Bangkok, Thailand

Thank you.

Minfong and Kwoncjan

86   7